"I'm just c

The sarcasm in her
recoil. "You've dec
with the ruthless logic you apply to everything else,
you decided I was the most likely candidate. I'm the
sister of your best friend, and you know I'm not
after your fortune. Your mother already loves me
like a daughter, so you have instant cooperation on
all fronts."

"Don't talk like a fool," Clint grated, his earlier
gentleness disappearing. "All this is just a smoke
screen for you to hide behind, Alicia."

"You don't understand me at all, do you?" she
asked, her eyes filling with tears.

"I understand you better than you do yourself," he
remarked coldly. "Isn't it about time you stopped
competing with the boys and let yourself be a
woman?"

"Why?" Alicia snapped. "So you can use your
sexual skill to keep me in my place? What better
weapon to use against me than my desire for you!
But you're not going to get the chance. When I
marry, it will be to a man who views me as his equal,
and I'll never settle for anything less...."

Dear Reader:

Happy holidays! All the best wishes to you for a joyful, loving holiday season with your family and friends.

And while celebrating, I hope that you think of Silhouette Romance. Our authors join me in wishing you a wonderful holiday season, and we have some treats in store for you during November and December—as well as during the exciting new year.

Experience the magic that makes the world so special for two people falling in love. Meet heroines who will make you cheer for their happiness and heroes (be they the boy next door or a handsome, mysterious stranger) who will win your heart. Silhouette Romances reflect the magic of love—sweeping you away with books that will make you laugh and cry, heartwarming, poignant stories that will move you time and time again.

During the next months, we're publishing romances by many of your all-time favorites such as Diana Palmer, Brittany Young, Lucy Gordon and Victoria Glenn. Your response to these authors and others in Silhouette Romances has served as a touchstone for us, and we're pleased to bring you more books with Silhouette's distinctive medley of charm, wit and—above all—*romance*.

I hope you enjoy this book and the many stories to come. Come home to Silhouette romance—for always!

Sincerely,

Tara Hughes
Senior Editor
Silhouette Books

NICOLE MONET

Guardian Angel

Silhouette *Romance*

Published by Silhouette Books New York

America's Publisher of Contemporary Romance

For Alicia Condon: Thanks for all the years of
friendship and for everything I learned from you.
By the way... this time your name is the
heroine's... not the other woman's!

SILHOUETTE BOOKS
300 E. 42nd St., New York, N.Y. 10017

ISBN: 0-373-08615-6

First Silhouette Books printing November 1988

Printed in the U.S.A.

NICOLE MONET,

an inveterate writer of romance, lives in California with her husband and daughter and makes of her writing a full-time career. "I write," the author says, "because I am a voracious reader, and I feel that in some small way, I'm paying back all the pleasure I've received in my lifetime."

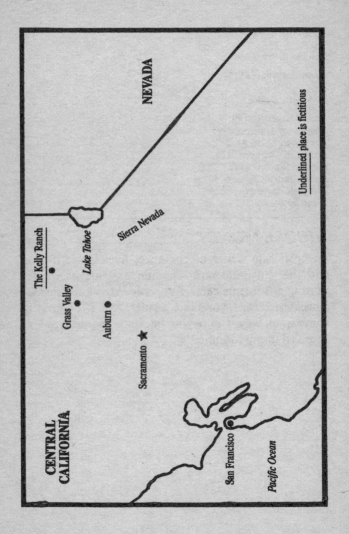

CENTRAL CALIFORNIA

NEVADA

The Kelly Ranch

Grass Valley

Auburn

Sacramento

Lake Tahoe

Sierra Nevada

San Francisco

Pacific Ocean

Underlined place is fictitious

Chapter One

Alicia Mason's footsteps were light and energetic as she crossed the graveled parking lot and entered the central offices of SafetyCo, the business she owned jointly with her brother, Kevin, and his wife, Jane. Her eyes took in the comfortable seating arrangements on either side of her as she passed through the maroon-carpeted foyer and she felt justifiably proud of all her family had accomplished during the past few years.

SafetyCo provided Grass Valley, Auburn and surrounding areas with efficient home security systems and trained guards to protect commercial property. The huge, gray building, located on the eastern boundary of Grass Valley, had been an abandoned warehouse until the Mason clan bought and remodeled it to suit their needs.

The business venture had been a sound one, especially for her. As teenagers, Kevin and his best friend Clint had signed up for karate instruction and preteen Alicia had watched with the hungry intensity of a natural athlete while they practiced. She had begun to emulate their graceful movements, much to Kevin's amusement and Clint's disgust. Eventually she had nagged her parents into letting her take lessons and within a few months she'd been promoted to the intermediate class.

Alicia smiled impishly as she remembered the look on Clint's face when the instructor had introduced her to the rest of the group. Clint had promptly quit the program, but as Alicia's skill had increased Kevin had become delighted with her progress. Although his own interest in karate had waned with Clint's defection, he'd convinced their parents to allow her to join local and later state competitions. Looking back, she couldn't help but wonder if she'd excelled as a competitor more to make her brother proud of her or more to irritate Clint.

Until Kevin had discussed his plans to open SafetyCo, she had looked upon her skills as a hobby. Once the idea of teaching martial arts came to her she was no longer in doubt as to the career she wished to follow. Of course Alicia hadn't been able to foresee the complications working with her brother would cause in her life. He had been her guardian since their parents had died when she was fourteen and, as nearly ten years separated them, he had always taken his responsibilities seriously. Too seriously, she decided, since the role of protector was one he seemed determined never to relinquish.

Alicia supposed his attitude was understandable since she'd spent her formative years following him around like an adoring puppy. She smiled wryly and rubbed the bunched muscles forming in the back of her neck. Just thinking about her stubborn, opinionated brother made her tense. Having him underfoot day in and day out was proving to be more of a nuisance than she'd ever imagined. What she had to do was find some way to make Kevin realize she needed to control her own life—before she had a nervous breakdown from all his well-intentioned interference.

Pushing aside an all too familiar feeling of aggravation, she gave her sister-in-law a beaming smile and a wave as she sauntered past the reception desk. If the number of lights blinking on the switchboard was any indication, Jane was too busy to stop and chat. Alicia gave a mental shrug of regret and continued down the back hallway toward the office she shared with her brother.

She was just reaching for the doorknob when she heard her name mentioned. She stiffened at the cold implacability in Kevin's voice. The door wasn't closed all the way and her ears twitched with the zeal of a dyed-in-the-wool eavesdropper as she leaned forward to peer through the crack. Her brother was seated at his desk, a scowl on his handsome face as he held the phone receiver to his ear. Then she heard him mutter, "I'm glad you and I have reached an understanding, Mr. Keel."

Alicia gasped in disbelief. She ought to strangle her overprotective sibling with his own tie. Charlie Keel was the man she'd been dating for several weeks and as Kevin continued to speak to him in hatefully sarcastic tones she stood frozen in place. What in heaven's name did her brother think he was doing? How dare he give poor Charlie the third degree? she asked herself incredulously. He was acting like some suspicious father in a Victorian melodrama.

Pure, blind fury released Alicia from her stunned state. She rushed into the room with murder in her eyes and grabbed the receiver out of Kevin's hand. But the damage had already been done. Charlie sounded nervous and subdued when she asked why he'd called. She was sure he'd been planning to ask her out but instead he made up a rather lame excuse and stammered an apology for disturbing her at work. Her heart sank. Well, she thought despondently, so much for a meaningful relationship with Charlie Keel. Since he seemed pathetically anxious to end their conversation, she let him off the hook with as cheerful a goodbye as she could manage through clenched teeth.

Alicia didn't want to let Kevin know his gestapo tactics had worked, but as she hung up the phone she felt humiliated as well as angry. When she glared across the desk to meet her brother's impassive gaze, she felt as if she'd been plugged into a high-voltage electrical conduit.

"What in the world did you think you were doing, Kevin?"

He clasped his hands behind his head. "I just answered the phone," he replied with maddening evasiveness, "and took the opportunity to introduce myself to your boyfriend."

"You mean you took the opportunity to intimidate him, don't you?"

His eyelashes flickered. "Is that what he told you?"

"He didn't have to." Alicia began to pace rapidly back and forth in front of his desk, the sound of her sandal heels tapping against the linoleum floor in imitation of the jumbled thoughts clicking away in her brain. "You had poor Charlie so shaken he couldn't tell me much of anything."

"I gather he's not a very..." Kevin hesitated long enough for his mouth to twitch into a satisfied smile before drawling, "...umm, a very forceful personality."

Alicia stopped her prowling to confront him with a cynical smirk. "If you mean he's not an interfering bully like you, then you're right!"

Kevin lowered his arms. His lanky frame remained relaxed as he slumped deeper into the chair's cushioned seat. His smile held a definite trace of smugness as he said, "I didn't have to bully him, Alicia."

"What did you say to him?"

His gaze shifted evasively. "Look, I don't have time to go into this now. Clint should be arriving any minute to go over that security system we set up for him at the Drill Well main office. We're going to discuss the feasibility of expanding the computer capability to tie in with a new system at his eastern plant."

If he had hoped to distract her with a business discussion, his mention of that black-haired son of Satan with the wickedly seductive eyes had the opposite effect. Clint's features suddenly superimposed themselves over her brother's and she ground her teeth together in irritation. As though Kevin wasn't enough of a problem in her life, she also had Clinton Kelly to contend with. He was as bossy and interfering as her brother, but since his mother, Sarah, was her godmother, she couldn't very well ignore him. The two men were like a matched set, with Clint often encouraging Kevin's dictator tactics.

Alicia's eyes narrowed suspiciously. "Wouldn't it have been more practical for the two of you to meet at Drill Well, where you could refer to the office layout on the map Clint has on his wall?"

Kevin seemed to find the green felt blotter on his desk of immense interest. "Uhh, I think Clint has something he wants to talk over with you."

"Talk over, or badger me about?" Her eyes widened as a horrible thought entered her mind, and she didn't wait to give Kevin a chance to reply. Straightening her body to its full five feet nothing, she noticed the natural puckish curve of her brother's mouth deepen with amusement and let fly at him. "Was that why you were so rude on the phone just now? If you've been discussing Charlie with Clint I'll kill you, Kevin Mason. My relationships with other men are no business of yours or his. I'm old enough not to have my boyfriends vetted, and I'm not going to stand interference from either of you."

Kevin gave a disgusted snort. "What relationship, Alicia? That jerk's a pantywaist without an ounce of backbone, or hadn't that occurred to you yet? When I told him he'd better be careful with you if he wanted to go on breathing he practically had a heart attack over the phone."

"You told him what?" Alicia screeched.

Kevin glared at her defiantly. "You heard me."

"What in the world possessed you to do such a thing, or did Clint put you up to it?"

A hectic flush colored his cheeks and his mouth formed a forbidding line. "You've got Clint all wrong, Alicia."

This time it was her turn to give a fulsome snort. "Don't you dare sit there and defend Clinton Kelly to me, Kevin. He's no better than you are. You both think just because I'm built like a damned pixie that I'm never going to grow up, but I've got news for you . . . I'm no Peter Pan!"

Kevin jumped to his feet. "No, you're just a little idiot who's too blind to see what's in front of her face. Don't you know that Clint—" He bit his words off abruptly and rubbed the back of his neck as he stared at her in a silence fraught with tension.

"Clint what?" she pressed belligerently.

"He . . . cares about you."

Kevin's vague response held a hesitation that puzzled her. "So do you," she interjected bitterly. "But that doesn't give either of you the right to interfere in my life."

"But Clint wants . . ."

"He wants what?" she asked with growing impatience.

His expression became guarded. "You'll know soon enough, Alicia."

"Will you stop speaking in riddles and half sentences, Kevin?"

Kevin bent forward and placed both palms on the desk top, his expression pleading. "Why don't you quit with the sarcasm and realize that I only have your best interests at heart, honey?''

When she remained stubbornly silent, he once again straightened to his full height. Alicia averted her eyes, resenting the psychological advantage towering over her gave him. God, she hated big men who refused to take her seriously because of her size. In fact she hated big men, period! With Kevin and Clint for examples, it was no wonder she was a firm believer in Women's Lib.

When she turned her pensive gaze back to Kevin, she almost groaned aloud. The hurt look on his face was one she was all too familiar with. He was usually able to use it effectively to make her feel too guilty to be as assertive as her independent nature demanded. For love of her Kevin had given up a great deal of his youth as well as the army career he'd always dreamed about. And the knowledge of his sacrifice was what now made it virtually impossible to fight his intrusion into her private life. But for once she wasn't going to let her love for him weaken her resistance, she decided, her chin angling upward in resolution.

''This time you're not getting away with it, Kevin.''

''Away with what?'' At the false innocence in his voice her ire returned with such force she thought she'd explode. As she studied her brother's features she wondered how such a possessive tyrant could appear so boyishly innocent. She quickly came to the conclusion that the freckles spread so generously across his well-shaped nose were at fault.

"You're not going to play on my emotions to make me feel like an uncaring witch. I respect you and value your approval but not at the expense of my pride and independence. Can't you see that your constant vigilance is stifling me?"

"I'm your brother, Alicia. Who's going to look out for you if I don't?"

"When will you realize that I can take care of myself? I appreciated your care when I was a child, Kevin. But now I'm a responsible adult with a right to privacy, not the little girl who used to tag along after you. This incident with Charlie Keel is the last straw. I'm warning you, I'm not putting up with this kind of interference any longer."

Alicia might as well have butted her head against a brick wall for all the attention her brother paid to her declaration of independence. He voiced his opinion of what he referred to as her "pigheadedness," and she retaliated hotly. Their argument went from bad to worse until their voices nearly blasted the plaster off the walls. By the time he stormed out of the office her eyes were filled with frustrated tears because she felt guilty and defiant at the same time.

A faint knock drew her gaze to the slowly opening door. Her sister-in-law's head peeked around the corner. "Is it safe to come in?"

Alicia's laugh sounded decidedly shaky. "Your husband and I have taken a time-out to plan our battle strategy."

"Uh-oh," Jane remarked as she settled her thin body on the edge of Alicia's desk. "I take it the war's not over."

"Is it ever?" Alicia countered glumly, plopping down in her chair with a weary sigh.

"I hate to say I told you so, but I warned you not to let Kevin know that your boyfriend was your next-door neighbor. After the fuss he made when you insisted on moving into your own apartment I knew he was going to hit the roof."

"I don't see what difference it makes, unless he thinks having Charlie so conveniently close is too much of a temptation for me."

Jane's head cocked to one side like an inquisitive blackbird's. "And is it?"

"If you knew Charlie you wouldn't have to ask," Alicia admitted with a disgruntled grimace.

"Then end the cold war and introduce him to Kevin."

"Brother dear would still scare him to death."

"Do you want a man who can be so easily intimidated?" Jane inquired with a moue of distaste.

"Yes...no...oh, that's not the point!" The downward curve of Alicia's mouth betrayed her pain. "Why can't he just trust me, Janey?"

The other woman gave her a bracing smile. "It's the men you date he doesn't trust."

Alicia bristled defensively. "He knows I can take care of myself if push comes to shove."

"Maybe he thinks you're overconfident."

"And maybe he just has a suspicious mind," Alicia retorted caustically. "But then, why wouldn't he? Until he met you he went through more women than a sultan with a harem. Oh, he tried to hide his lustful tendencies from his innocent little sister," she said with a grin, "but I had a spy network to rival James Bond."

"He did have quite a reputation," Jane agreed. "That's why I wouldn't date him for so long."

"Thank goodness you finally gave in," Alicia responded with heartfelt sincerity. "Although taking on my brother and a rebellious sixteen year old should have made you prematurely gray."

Jane ran a hand over her short, straight black hair and chuckled. "The two of you weren't so bad, especially once I'd gotten over the hurdle of accepting Kevin's proposal. My father thought I had a screw loose and when I stopped to think about it I almost agreed with him. Which just goes to show you..."

"What, that you had bats in your belfry?" Alicia interrupted.

Jane shook a fist in her direction but her thin features shone with good humor. "I was going to remind you that even your stubborn brother can change.''

Alicia's answering smile didn't reach her eyes. ''Where you're concerned maybe, but I've given up hope for myself. I've heard reformed rakes make the best husbands, but they make rotten brothers, Janey.''

With a sympathetic look in Alicia's direction Jane got gracefully to her feet and stretched. As she slowly pivoted on her spike heels and headed for the door, she murmured a parting bit of advice over her shoulder. ''Just keep slugging, Chickie, and eventually you'll win the war of equality.''

After Jane left, an annoying voice from Alicia's subconscious began to mock her. Was that why she'd ignored Jane's warning and deliberately let Kevin know that Charlie was her next-door neighbor as well as her boyfriend? Had her yearning to be respected as an adult caused her to force her brother's hand just to see how he would react? Well, she was no longer in any doubt as to how far Kevin would go to protect her virtue, she decided wrathfully. He would stop at nothing to keep her under his thumb, even if his actions resulted in her complete and total mortification.

With an impatient grimace Alicia pulled the brown account ledger from her desk drawer and plopped it down in front of her. Grabbing a pencil from the ceramic holder on her desk, she began to nibble the end of the eraser. Her thoughts were jumbled and inconsistent and, as she withdrew the gnawed pencil from her mouth, she disgustedly studied the teeth marks on what was left of the eraser. Sitting around mulling over her problems wasn't getting her anywhere. She had classes scheduled for the afternoon and the accountant was coming tomorrow to go over the books with her. She had to bring them up-to-date and if she didn't get a move on she'd be here half the night.

The clock on the office wall caught Alicia's attention, the bold, black hands against its white face reminding her how much of the morning had been wasted arguing. With a sigh she bent her head and began to work, but her preoccupation was a definite deterrent to accuracy. By the time both hands on the clock were pointing toward the ceiling, her jaw ached from clenching her teeth and the flushed color in her cheeks matched her flaming curls. When she added the ledger column for the third time and got still another unlikely total, she leaned back in her chair and uttered a few choice words to convey her disgust.

"Hi, Angel Face," drawled a deep voice that held an undercurrent of laughter. "Sounds like you need your mouth washed out with soap."

Only one man called her that, and the sound of Clinton Kelly's husky tones did nothing to restore her equilibrium or her good manners. "What do you want?"

Her rudeness caused a slight grin to tease one corner of his mouth, and the odd curling sensation she felt in her stomach didn't do much for her temper. She was just hungry, she decided. Without taking her eyes off Clint's bold, harshly defined features, she grabbed a shiny red apple from the top of her desk and sank her teeth into it. Although the juice eased the dryness of her throat, the snack was curiously tasteless and she chewed the succulent fruit without interest.

Clint's black eyes sparkled wickedly as he leaned his broad shoulders against the edge of the doorway and watched her. His voice took on a husky vibrancy as he murmured, "Are you really ready to hear what I want, Alicia?"

When she tried to swallow, a piece of apple went down the wrong way and she glared at him as she choked. Ever since she'd had that disastrous crush on him when she was younger she'd felt uneasy in his presence, but at least she'd stopped blushing when he turned those long-lashed bedroom eyes of his in her direction. Thank heaven she was no longer susceptible to the sensual allure that had once blinded her to his true nature, she told herself bracingly.

By the time she'd finished coughing, the deep resonance of his laughter filled the room. With streaming eyes she stared from him to the apple clenched in her hand, her intention obvious. "Will you stop laughing at me?"

"What will you do?" he asked mockingly. "Break my nose? Unless you've forgotten, Kevin already beat you to it when we were in high school. That's what comes of fighting over a female."

Mention of her brother fanned her simmering temper and she snapped, "Then I'll break it again before I go after him."

Clint ran a hand over his mouth but didn't quite manage to subdue his widening grin. "Ahh, I take it he's in trouble again."

Alicia's chin rose. "It's none of your business."

"Of course it is," he corrected with an air of injured innocence. "You're my godsister, aren't you?"

"Your mother is my godmother but you were not part of a package deal," she muttered. "How someone as sweet as Sarah could have given birth to such a pain in the—"

"She loves me," he interrupted smugly before she could describe him to her satisfaction, "and don't swear. It isn't ladylike."

Alicia jumped to her feet. "I'm no lady, you pompous, ignorant, chauvinistic..." Her chest heaved as she struggled to catch her breath. "You're as blind as my brother and twice as obstinate. You both think you can walk all over me, but you and Kevin are in for a rude awakening, Clint."

"We've been in for it since the day you were born, you little firebrand." He shook his head reprovingly. "You certainly live up to that red hair of yours."

She tried to focus on her martial arts training, which stressed personal discipline. With as much dignity as she could muster she responded shakily, "My hair is not red. It's strawberry blond. Kevin's the carrot top in our family."

"Red is red," he remarked dryly, "and you both have tempers to match. What's he done to get you into a snit this time?"

Alicia told him, her mutinous glare daring him to laugh. Although she thought she saw his lips twitch, his response succeeded in soothing some of her irritation. "Kev shouldn't have embarrassed you like that. It seems you have a legitimate gripe this time."

"You bet I do," she snapped. "Just because Charlie lives in the apartment next to mine, Kevin imagines we're playing musical beds."

Clint tensed and his indulgent smile disappeared with a swiftness that left her gasping. "Is it all in his imagination, Alicia?"

Hearing the suspicion in his voice was the last straw, and the partially eaten apple she was still holding went sailing through the air. "You go to hell, Clinton Kelly," she yelled furiously. "I'm quite capable of managing my own affairs."

Clint dodged and the missile sailed past him. As he straightened he fixed her with a brooding stare, his voice heavy with repressed violence as he repeated, "Affairs?"

"Why so shocked?" she inquired sarcastically. "You have them so why shouldn't I? I'm a grown woman and we do have equal rights these days."

The piercing blackness of his eyes burned a derisive path from the top of her head to the tips of her toes. "Then you should try curbing that wicked temper of yours and act like one."

She stared at him defiantly. "Your idea of a woman and mine are vastly different, Mr. Kelly. I'm not the simpering, fawning type. I'll never pander to any man's ego, especially yours. Macho men leave me cold."

"Shall we put it to the test?"

As he straightened there was a new look in his eyes, a burning intensity she didn't much care for. Alicia swallowed nervously as he began to move toward her with the sinuous grace of a sleek and deadly predator. She wasn't worried, she assured herself as she began to back away from her desk. After all, she'd thrown guys nearly double her weight onto the practice mat. Yes, that inner voice reminded her with a cowardice she deplored, but this particular man was built like a damned mountain.

"It's no w-wonder you and Kevin have been friends all your lives," she stammered defensively, her breath catching in her throat when she bumped into the wall and came to an abrupt halt. "You're both too certain of your male superiority to consider my feelings."

He stopped less than two feet away from her, his expression guarded. "I've tried to stay your friend, too, but you've become adept at avoiding me."

She gave him a startled glance from beneath her thick fringe of lashes and he laughed humorlessly. "Do you think I haven't noticed? Even my mother has caught on over the past few years, since the only time you visit the ranch anymore is when you know I'm out of town."

"I'm not the one who's gone most of the time," she snapped. "Are you certain you're not the one doing the avoiding?"

"Is that what you really think?" he murmured softly.

Alicia lowered her head to avoid his questioning gaze and immediately wished she hadn't. Her attention was caught by shoulders that had to measure three feet across. She took in the thatch of black, curly hair that showed through the open neck of his snugly fitting Western shirt.

When she was younger she'd spent many a hot summer day swimming with Clint and Kevin in Clint's parents' pool, and she couldn't help recalling how that dark, luxurious mat spread across his chest and narrowed to a vee when it reached his hard, flat stomach. She shivered at the memory and despised herself for the betraying tremor that raised goose-flesh on her skin.

His scent drifted across the distance separating them—a mingling of soap, the spicy after-shave he preferred and warm male flesh. Clint brushed his hands against the wall on either side of her head and she flinched. She felt a sensual hunger that a mere apple wouldn't appease, but it was a response she did her best to hide. She didn't like feeling vulnerable to this man, although it had been the case for more years than she wanted to admit.

When he had kissed her on her sixteenth birthday she'd felt her first taste of desire and had become obsessed with the longing to repeat the experience. He had barely brushed her mouth with his, but it had been enough to forever destroy the easy relationship she'd always known with him. For weeks she had made every excuse in the book to be with him, her need glaringly obvious to anyone who cared to look.

Alicia felt humiliated by the vividness of her memories and she fought against the urge to hide her face from him. Self-contempt replaced courage as she forced herself to meet his eyes. She could see herself in their depths and the illusion seemed strangely intimate. Her heart began to thud against the wall of her chest and she thought she'd suffocate if he came any closer. There didn't seem to be enough air in the room to allow her to breathe and she could almost feel her confidence slipping away.

Desperately seeking a change of subject she used his reference to his mother to distract him. "Is Sarah over her cold yet?" she inquired nervously. "I haven't had a chance to talk to her this week."

Momentarily diverted, Clint frowned and nodded. "She's better physically, but I'm worried about her, Alicia."

"What's wrong?" she asked, alarmed at his serious tone.

He shook his head impatiently and shrugged. "We've been getting some crank calls and you know how nervous she is under the best of circumstances."

"You shouldn't leave her alone so much. She hates being by herself at night in that big house."

"I've got a business to run," he reminded her brusquely. "Mother has my foreman and his wife less than half a mile away. All she has to do is call them if she gets anxious."

"You know Sarah's too proud to admit her fears."

His eyes narrowed as he studied her disapproving features. "To anyone but you."

"I'm her goddaughter," she retorted indignantly. "Of course she confides in me."

"Then if she mentions these damned phone calls to you, will you try to calm her down? She's becoming paranoid."

"I'll do my best, but does she have reason to be frightened, Clint?"

His eyes became shuttered as he stared into the distance. "Somebody with a grudge is trying to make my life miserable. It's no more than a simple case of verbal intimidation, but you know what Mother's like."

"You *are* her only son," Alicia reminded him curtly. "She worries about you."

He grinned. "She worries about you even more than she does me."

Alicia's features softened. "I know and I love her for it."

"I worry about you," he admitted softly. "Do you love me, too?"

She gave him a killing glance. "Sarah is lovable; you are merely provoking."

"And there's no one she'd rather see me leg-shackled to than you, or hasn't that crossed your mind yet?"

Her voice rose a full decibel as her eyes flashed a warning. "You don't have to worry about losing your bachelor status, Mr. Kelly. You're too old to interest me."

"I was too old when you were sixteen," he murmured, leaning forward until his warm, minty breath made her lips tingle, "but you're a woman now, or so you claim. If it's an affair you're after, why don't you choose me over this Charlie character?"

She gasped at his audacity. "Unlike you, I don't indulge in affairs!"

Alicia almost groaned aloud. In her haste to defend herself she'd played right into Clint's hands, she realized in disgust. He'd wanted to know if her relationship with Charlie had gone beyond friendship and now he had his answer. When was she going to learn not to let her temper rule her tongue? she wondered despairingly.

She was torn by conflicting emotions. Although she didn't want to admit it, she was more hurt than angered by Clint's baiting. He knew she could never match him for sophistication and experience, and he had deliberately used his undoubted sensuality to satisfy his curiosity. What hurt the most was his ruthlessness in achieving his own ends. He was taunting her with his knowledge of what she'd once felt for him; making a mockery of those pitifully young, tender emotions to teach her a lesson. She gripped her hands together at her waist, determined to mask her distress from him. If there were any lessons to be learned, she vowed silently, he was going to be the one to learn them.

Chapter Two

Alicia was proud of the cool composure in her manner as she searched Clint's features unflinchingly. "I think you get entirely too much pleasure out of teasing me. Why don't you go torment one of the leggy blondes who find you so irresistible?"

To her amazement his eyes flashed with something closely resembling regret. "You've never forgiven me for that night, have you, honey?"

Alicia lowered her lashes to hide the sudden anguish his question had caused. The night he was referring to had occurred less than a month after that momentous kiss, and she didn't want to think about the stupid, crazily infatuated girl she'd been. She winced inwardly as she remembered how eagerly she'd accepted Clint's invitation to spend the weekend with him and his mother while Kevin was away on business. She had been filled with youthful hopefulness, completely unaware of the agony in store for her.

"I don't know what you're talking about," she replied stiltedly.

Clint's response was swift and merciless and without concern for her obvious embarrassment. "Answer my question, Alicia. Or shall I do it for you?"

"There was nothing to forgive," she said with touching dignity. "You had every right to invite your girlfriend to dinner."

His thick hair fell over his forehead and he pushed it back impatiently. "I know, but I've never been able to forget the shattered look on your face when I walked in with Paula. I'd invited her over that night to make a point, not to humiliate you."

Alicia prayed that she didn't appear as sickened by the memory as she felt. "You just wanted to show me how foolish I was to imagine you might be interested in me, when there were beautiful, sophisticated women like Paula around."

"But I hadn't meant to so completely disillusion you." His voice was filled with contrition, his expression tender as he looked at her. "I'd forgotten what a sensitive little romantic you were."

"Well, I'm not any longer," she remarked with a cynicism she didn't entirely feel.

"Like hell you're not!"

Obviously Clint wasn't in the least impressed by her sarcasm. If the way he was glaring at her was any indication, he'd like to wring her neck. The impression gave Alicia a great deal of satisfaction, but the coiled tension of his body decided her against goading him any further. With assumed nonchalance she shrugged her shoulders and stared with pointed intensity at the deep cleft in his chin. "I don't know what you're getting so uptight about. That night served the purpose you intended and I got over my blind infatuation in record time."

"But I wasn't prepared to have you turn away from me so completely. We'd always been close, especially after your mom and dad were killed."

Alicia froze at the wave of pain that still came with the memory. She had been staying with her godparents when her parents had taken that last, fatal journey together in her father's plane. They had taken off from Auburn's small airport, headed for Lake Tahoe to enjoy a second honeymoon. That evening Clint had come to Alicia's for dinner. On the six o'clock news, Clint and Alicia had heard of the crash of a Cessna en route to Tahoe. No details had been given.

It had been Clint's hand Alicia had clung to after he'd called the local authorities for information and had discovered that it was, in fact, her father's plane that had gone down in the mountains. He was the

one who sat with her while they waited for a report
from the air rescue team. When they found out there
were no survivors, it was Clint she'd turned to while
she screamed and cried in an agony of grief.

The touch of Clint's hand against her face brought
her back to the present. "I valued the affection we
always shared," he said solemnly, "and having you
treat me like a pariah all these years has been hard to
take."

Alicia swallowed past the lump in her throat. His
sincere admission so quickly following the memory
of that terrible night was almost more than she could
bear. She could feel moisture filling her eyes and her
heart was aching with remorse. "I never thanked
you, did I?"

"For what, sweetheart?"

"For being there when I needed you," she whispered.

A gentle smile curved his mouth and his fingers
brushed away the single tear trailing down her cheek.
"You were there for me when my father died," he
reminded her softly. "You came into my study and
knelt at my feet. Do you remember?"

She nodded and remarked shyly, "I held your
hand."

"Yes." The expression on his face conveyed such
a depth of emotion she couldn't stop staring at him.
"You didn't say a word. You didn't have to. I could
feel your love surrounding me, Angel Face. You

eased the pain I was feeling and gave me the strength to face my loss.

"Oh, God, Alicia," he groaned suddenly. "You're a part of me. Don't you realize that? This distance you've placed between us is so unnecessary—so painful to us both. You're not sixteen anymore. Isn't it time you forgave the hurt I caused you?"

Her laughter was completely lacking in amusement. "At least you made me stop making a nuisance of myself."

"You were never a nuisance," he murmured quietly. "You were just too damned young for the kind of games you were playing."

"You think I was playing?" she asked, all too aware of the bitter inflection in her voice. "If so, I certainly didn't enjoy myself."

With nerve-shattering tenderness he brushed her taut jawline with the back of his hand, and her eyes widened incredulously when he said, "Then maybe it's time you did, Angel."

Clint's meaning couldn't have been clearer if he'd branded it on her forehead in letters of fire, but her mind refused to accept what her ears had heard. "What are you saying?"

Her voice was faint and the shock that must have been evident in her eyes made his features harden with resolution. "I think you know the answer to that."

Alicia tried to speak but her lips felt stiff and oddly uncoordinated. Tentatively touching her mouth with the tip of her tongue, she swept her gaze upward to his face. She drew in a deep breath, barely managing to choke out a denial. "I don't know what you're talking about."

"I want us to be together," he said with a composure that lent credence to his words. "I've felt that way for years, only you were too young to know your own mind. Why do you think I used Paula to discourage you? Hell, I was finding it pretty nearly impossible not to destroy your illusions along with my own self-respect. Every time you peeked up at me with those big, haunting eyes of yours I saw myself as a white knight, when I knew I was really the dragon. I didn't want you blinded by hero worship, so I was forced to wait until you grew up enough to see me as a man with human needs and failings."

Alicia shook her head, bewildered by the enormity of this situation. If he was saying what she thought he was, Kevin would kill him! At the thought she felt the urge to laugh, but she knew giving in to the hysterical giggle building in her throat would almost definitely be ill-advised. If the look in Clint's eyes meant anything, this was definitely the time to use some measure of diplomacy in her dealings with him. Especially since she was having the greatest difficulty believing what he was telling her.

"I...I don't appreciate th-this kind of humor, Clinton."

Her use of his full name caused a grin, albeit a taut one, to curve his mouth. Her head was thrown back and his glance lingered against her arched throat, then lifted to encompass her rebellious features. He tangled his mobile fingers in her red-gold hair, then leaned forward to brush her parted lips with a soft kiss. "I've never been more serious in my life, Alicia."

How does he do it? she asked herself in panic-stricken dismay. Her silent question seemed to escalate the swift flame of desire that pulsed through her body, started by the touch of his lips against her own. In spite of her brother's vigilance she'd dated quite a bit in her twenty-three years and received her share of kisses, some of them given by experts. Although she'd sometimes felt mild pleasure, not once had she considered letting those forgotten men lead her into further experimentation.

Yet all Clint had to do was breathe on her, she thought incredulously, and she stopped thinking rationally. No longer was she controlled and level-headed. Instead she was confused by this abrupt change in his attitude and uncertain of what he expected of her. She thought of all the women like Paula in his past, women who were experienced and self-assured. How could she ever hope to satisfy a sensual man like Clint when just the thought terrified her?

He viewed the deepening color in her cheeks before his attention returned to the pulse pounding in her throat. This symptom of her vulnerability seemed to anger him and he uttered a mild expletive as he pushed himself away from her. She jumped at the suddenness of his withdrawal and stared at his back in dismay. Clint straightened and brushed at his hair with restless fingers as he turned to face her.

"Damn it, Alicia," he finally ground out. "Don't look at me like that."

She jerked guiltily and her gaze skittered away from the knowing look in his eyes. She flushed an even rosier hue and mumbled weakly, "Like what?"

"Like you expect me to jump on you at any moment," he retorted grimly. "I'm not a patient man but I intend to give you enough time to accept the changes in our relationship."

She gazed at him pleadingly. "Clint, this has gone far enough."

"Then you have no conception of distance, baby."

"I'm not a baby!" The indignant exclamation was a mere sop to her pride, when secretly the husky endearment pleased her enormously. It had been spoken in his liquid-honey voice, which had the power to melt all her defenses. As she watched him her delicate features were preoccupied, her mind trying desperately to gain control over her fluctuating emotions.

"But you're not yet as wordly as you'd have me believe," he whispered softly. "Are you, Alicia?"

To avoid answering she glanced past him to the sandals tucked beneath her desk. She felt gauche and childish standing in her bare feet and she wished she hadn't given in to habit and kicked the sandals off. For lack of a more appropriate distraction she concentrated on the tips of her toes, but their nakedness in transparent nylons only served as an unwanted reminder of her wayward thoughts.

She listened to the exasperated hiss of his indrawn breath with quivering trepidation. The sound seemed to echo against the walls and contrasted sharply with the silence that had followed his question. It was so quiet she could even hear the monotonous ticking of the clock overhead. Realizing how much time had passed since he'd spoken caused a reaction in Alicia she regretted, but couldn't resist. On more than one occasion in her life her rampant curiosity had gotten her into trouble and she was almost certain this was going to be one of those times. But she had to see his expression or die of frustration, so she mentally braced herself to take the initiative.

Alicia didn't think there was anything remotely funny about her present circumstances, and when she saw the smile on Clint's mouth what little composure she had left was blown to smithereens. He was playing with her the way a cat does with a mouse before the kill. The realization lent a scathing revulsion to her low tones. "Get out of here before I do something we'll both regret, Clint."

Immediately his indulgent expression altered and his large frame tensed. "I always told Kevin it was a mistake to let you continue with those damned self-defense classes. Aggression in a woman is unbecoming and I'm getting damned sick and tired of it from you, Alicia."

"When will you get it through your thick skull that I don't particularly care what kind of opinion you have of me?"

"You care," he grated harshly. "You're just too immature to admit it."

"Don't you mean unfeminine?" she questioned sardonically.

His eyes raked over her body in a thoroughly masculine appraisal. "I wouldn't say that," he drawled lazily. "You're a tiny little thing but you've got everything in all the right places. You're exquisite, Angel."

She blinked. A feeling of unreality washed over her at her failure to react angrily to the suggestive mockery in his voice. She knew the way he was looking at her was disgusting, yet she couldn't seem to summon even a shred of indignation. Instead her knees seemed to be turning to rubber and her entire body was shaking with reaction.

"What, no snide comments, baby?"

This time the appellation was less of an endearment and more of an accusation. She drew in a strengthening breath and glared at him. "Just what do you expect from me?"

His eyes narrowed while his mouth took on a sensual cast that caught her unwilling attention the way a high-powered magnet drew steel. "I expect you to behave like a woman and not a child," he said.

Alicia tilted her chin imperiously, but her voice trembled as she remarked flatly, "You want an affair."

"I want to claim what belongs to me," he countered swiftly.

Her heart seemed to leap into her throat then settled back in her chest with a jolt. Her pulse hammered crazily, and she wondered if her nervous system could withstand many more shocks of this nature. "That's not true," she whispered.

"You've always belonged to me," he stated calmly. "I don't know when my feelings for you changed but I stopped viewing you as an honorary sister a long time ago. Maybe the catalyst was the look on your face when you saw me with Paula that night." He shook his head and gazed at her with rueful candor. "You made me feel ashamed, as though I had no right to be with another woman."

Since she'd felt much the same way herself, Alicia couldn't deny his allegation. In truth she didn't have the courage to try. But there was one thing she was going to make clear to him if it was the last thing she did. Straightening her spine to give the impression of a confidence she was far from feeling, she said firmly, "Your arrogant attitude stinks, Clint. The only person I belong to is myself."

His mouth twisted in derision. "Shall I prove how wrong you are, Angel Face?"

Her world seemed to tilt on its axis as he moved slowly toward her and her senses spun out of control when he slipped his hands from his pockets and reached for her. He cupped her face between his palms; the sensation of his flesh against her own was almost more than she could bear. Quickly she masked her alarm behind lowered lashes but even that avenue of escape was lost to her when he taunted, "Afraid to look at me?"

"I . . . I'm not. . . ."

Alicia's voice trailed off into nothingness as she became cocooned in a sensuality beyond her experience. She couldn't prevent her lashes from flickering upward and soon discovered her inability to escape the luring depths of his midnight eyes. They seemed to be weaving a spell around her, speaking to her of a touch she would soon welcome. The sensation of Clint's large hands cradling her cheeks while his thumbs probed the corners of her mouth was almost her undoing. She could imagine his warm, blunt-tipped fingers sliding down until they moved against her yielding body in masculine demand.

"You're so beautiful."

His comment sounded forced from him…almost bitter. Compulsively her gaze moved to his mouth in fascination. She was drowning beneath the undertow of his practiced seduction, and she didn't have the slightest will to resist. Before she could stop herself she leaned toward him, so drawn to his male aura she was mindless with the longing to press herself against his body's heat.

When the devastating tension increased between them, she realized instantly the magnitude of her error. He seemed barely controlled and she sensed an elemental force inside him, a raw power that had the ability to sap her will and destroy the person she'd fought so hard to become. She shivered in instinctive recoil. He was too much like Kevin in his attitudes, and for her to give in to her need for the physical assuagement he offered would be insane.

No matter how often she'd tried to deny the truth to herself in the past, she had loved Clint too long and too intensely to remain impervious to his domination. He would take over her life completely, she thought with a feeling of impending doom, because that was the kind of man he was. Although he'd often stated his belief in the equality of the sexes and had promoted women as well as men to executive positions in his corporation, it would be different with her.

Like her brother, Clint had considered himself her protector for too long to change now. No matter how much the realization hurt, she couldn't afford the risk of an intimate relationship with this man. Yet no matter how decisive her thoughts, she wasn't able to resist the sensual glow that seemed to emanate from the dark eyes that searched every inch of her face. She didn't have the strength to hide the trembling that started in the pit of her stomach and spread delicious tentacles of desire throughout her bloodstream.

Before she could stop herself, she whispered, "You're beautiful, too."

Clint gave her a satisfied smile. "I'm glad you think so."

Until this moment, she realized in amazement, she'd never completely understood his power over her senses. She was becoming lost to herself, and all the arguments her mind could summon against giving in to him were so much chaff blowing in the wind. The strength of the attraction she felt boggled her mind and she couldn't understand where all her resistance had gone. She tried to remember her need for protection against dominant men but her memory failed her when she needed it the most.

"Please don't do this to me."

Alicia hated herself for the piteousness of her plea and she was finally forced to accept what she'd denied for years. She wanted this man with a desperation that shamed her self-reliant nature, and yet she knew her need of him was a weakness she couldn't afford.

"I want you Alicia." The groaning reminder caused her to shake her head in violent negation, and his hands slipped away from her face.

"You . . . you've wanted other women," she reminded him in anguished tones. "Choose someone else to be your mistress."

"There is no one else."

Her lips curved cynically. "Tell it to the marines, Romeo."

Clint uttered a restrained laugh. "I admit there have been women in my past, but they were sophisticates who knew the score. It's taken you a hell of a long time to be ready for me, sweetheart."

"What makes you so certain I'm ready now?"

A muscle pulsed against the side of his jaw, his tension obvious. "His name is Charlie Keel."

"So I was right," she accused in sudden realization. "Kevin did blab to you, didn't he? What did he do—ask you to divert my attention by pretending an interest in me?"

"Your brother and I are friends but he wouldn't trust me with you any farther than he could throw me."

"That's because he knows you too well," she retorted.

"I had dinner with him and Jane last night," he continued stiffly. "Up until now you've never gone out with the same guy for very long so I wasn't worried. When Kevin mentioned you'd been dating that jerk for several weeks I decided I'd given you enough time, Alicia."

"Well, thank you very much for your patience," she snapped angrily. "Why didn't you just ask me if my relationship with Charlie was getting serious?"

"Because I didn't care whether it was serious or not." The harshness of his voice conveyed his pitiless obstinacy. "I'm damned if I'll stand by and let another man take you from me."

Alicia's eyes flashed, his possessiveness striking a death blow to any hopes for a future with him she might still have been harboring. It was obvious that she'd been right to be wary, because already Clint was denying her the right to choose her own path. He didn't care how she felt, not as long as he got his own way. Slowly her fingers dug into her palms, until tiny crescents appeared on the skin.

Taking him by surprise she lunged at him, pushing herself away from temptation with all the strength she could muster. She was halfway across the room before she turned and fixed him with a stare of pure rebellion. "I am not yours to take."

Clint's teeth ground together as he muttered, "You want me as much as I want you."

"It's time you learned that I make my own choices, Clint," she stated coldly. "I'm no man's plaything."

His smile seemed to hold a threatening element. "That's good, because I'm tired of Barbie Dolls."

Alicia slammed her clenched fists onto her slender hips and glared at him. "That's all women are to you, just toys. You take them out, play until you're bored and then discard them."

"But you see," he drawled, his determination clear in spite of his casual tone, "you've placed the wrong interpretation on my intentions, Alicia. I want more than an affair with you. I want you to be my wife."

"Wife?" she said incredulously. Her voice rose to a squeak as she anxiously questioned, "Did you say wife?"

"You didn't really believe there could be any other solution for us, did you?" He studied her dazed features and then grinned with sudden amusement. "I value my hide. If Kevin didn't murder me, my mother would."

It was the mention of her brother that finally dispelled the lingering wisps of confusion from Alicia's mind. With horror she took in the full message contained in Clint's backhanded proposal. He didn't really want to marry her, he just wanted her in his bed. Because of his close friendship with Kevin and her relationship with his mother, he was being forced to do the honorable thing to gain what he desired. His ruthlessness appalled her and made her more determined than ever to resist him.

"I'm not going to marry you, Clint. Not now. Not ever."

This time his smile was more mocking than amused. "We'll see, Angel Face."

"I mean it," she cried desperately. "I don't want to be your lover or your wife, Clint. I just want you to leave me alone."

He took a single step until their bodies touched, the look in his eyes resolute, his deep tones ravishing her senses. "I could change your mind, Alicia. You know that, don't you?"

"You'll never get the chance."

As she rushed out of the office, she thought she heard him mutter, "Never is a long time, Angel."

Alicia rested her elbow on the smooth wood grain of the patio table in front of her, her chin cupped in her palm. It was Jane's day off and she'd invited Alicia for lunch. They'd eaten outside on the wide, unpainted deck that ran across the back of Kevin's home at Lake of the Pines. Although the lofty evergreens Alicia loved were sparser here than in Grass Valley, there was still plenty of gorgeous foliage to enhance the brisk spring weather.

This was one of her favorite places to spend a relaxing afternoon, and usually she would have delighted in her surroundings. White fluffy clouds floated against the brilliance of the sky and were reflected in the cobalt-blue beauty of the lake. The sunshine turned her curls into an aureole of coppery red, the warmth pleasant against her scalp.

But her mood was far from pleasant as she stared at the shoreline. In her mind she was picturing Clint, every six-foot-four, muscular inch. More than a week had passed since he'd declared his intentions toward her and she couldn't seem to stop thinking about him. Her preoccupation made her madder than hell, even more at herself than at him.

At first she'd been afraid he would continue to try to wear down her defenses but when the days passed and he didn't return to torment her she'd been furious. The inconsistency of her emotions disgusted her and of course she blamed him for being the cause of her mental turmoil. He had about as much sincerity as a flea, she told herself. She was certain if he could see her now he would gain a great deal of enjoyment watching her itch.

Clint was playing a waiting game but he was going to be disappointed. There was no way she was going to calmly walk into the spider's web, and the sooner he realized that the better. Eventually he would set his sights on another, more suitable female, and she'd be free of him. Alicia scowled at the thought of him with another woman, but she knew it was inevitable. Clint was a man in every sense of the word and he wouldn't go into a decline and live like a monk because she had turned him down.

In fact that's probably why he hadn't been around. She wouldn't be surprised if he'd already lined up her successor, probably another luscious blonde with legs that went on forever. With a wry twist of her lips she glanced down at the bareness of her own legs below the blue exercise leotard cut high on her hips. She didn't appreciate the shapeliness of tanned muscle and bone but saw only the slenderness. As thin as two matchsticks, she decided with disgruntled inaccuracy.

Jane's amicably modulated voice brought Alicia's thoughts back from their meandering path. "Although I've enjoyed your visit enormously, don't you have a class to teach in less than an hour?"

Under the circumstances Alicia welcomed the distraction. She leaped from her chair with a dismayed exclamation. "My sauntering in late is hardly an example of the self-control I try to promote in my students."

Jane laughed affectionately and got to her feet to give Alicia a hug. "You've been about as controlled as a walking time bomb this afternoon. Are you still holding a grudge against Kevin for that stupid trick he pulled with your boyfriend? If so, the idiot deserves it. By the time I got through with him he was wishing he'd never been born."

"He's not the only one," Alicia grumbled as she stepped through the sliding glass doors and into the family room.

Jane followed her through the house to the front entry hall, and when Alicia turned she noticed the worried expression on the other woman's face. "Oh, don't listen to me," Alicia pleaded, waving her hand in a gesture of exasperation. "I don't know what's wrong with me lately."

Jane was immediately reassured and she smiled slyly. "Maybe you're in love."

Alicia's whole body jerked to attention as she practically shouted, "Why would you think that?"

"Forbidden fruit is sweeter," she teased. "Hasn't Kevin's disapproval made Charlie Keel seem like the passion of your life?"

Alicia almost sagged with relief. In loftily superior accents she informed the grinning countenance next to her of her determination to ignore the entire male species. Jane's smile widened. "Does that include your brother?" she asked.

"He's a man, isn't he?"

"A man who loves you very much," Jane reminded her.

Giving her a ruefully apologetic grimace, Alicia nodded. "I know that and I love him, too. It's just that lately I seem to have lost my sense of perspective along with my sense of humor.''

"Then it's a good thing you're finally taking a vacation," Jane retorted. "A month away from Kevin will give you a little breathing space. Have you decided where you're going, yet?"

"I'm hungry for the sight of the ocean," Alicia admitted with a sigh of anticipation, "so I've reserved a cabin at Santa Cruz for a few days. Other than that I refuse to make any plans. I want to feel free and unhampered by routine for a change. I only wish I didn't have another week and a half before I can leave."

"You've got the Memorial Day weekend coming up," Jane said soothingly. "You mentioned earlier that Sarah had invited you out to the ranch. It will do you good to get away."

"I don't know if I'm going," she remarked casually. "I invited Sarah to come and stay with me instead."

"But you love it there," Jane protested, her expression puzzled.

Alicia studiously avoided looking directly at her sister-in-law. "You know Clint and I are like oil and water," she remarked with assumed unconcern. "We just don't mix."

Jane cleared her throat and bent down to pluck a few weeds from the flower bed bordering the front lawn. "Didn't Sarah mention that Clint left a few days ago on another business trip? He's not expected back until after the holiday.''

Alicia had moved past Jane to begin descending the front steps, but at her sister-in-law's words she turned and almost pitched headfirst into Jane's beloved dahlias. So that's why he hadn't been around making her life miserable, she thought. He could have told her he was going away and saved her all the anxiety she'd suffered these past few days waiting for him to pounce, but turning her into a nervous wreck had probably been his intention all along.

Drumming up her anger, Alicia refused to acknowledge the relief she felt knowing he hadn't just changed his mind about her. It took a lot of effort but she managed to sound cool and collected when she said, "Sarah never mentioned any business trip.''

"Oh, well," Jane responded. "She probably didn't know Clint would be away when she invited you. He was supposed to play golf with Kevin earlier this week and called to cancel at the last minute. I take it some crisis blew up at one of their eastern factories.''

"That sounds like Clinton," Alicia exclaimed indignantly. "He cares more for that corporation of his than he does for his mother.''

"He has responsibilities," Jane said in gentle reproof. "You know if it were up to him he wouldn't leave the ranch, but his father left him in charge of

Drill Well and there are a lot of people depending on him for work.''

By this time they had reached the driveway, and Alicia kicked at the ground with the edge of her sandal. She winced when a few pieces of gravel lodged under her toes but decided it served her right for giving in to the childish impulse. "He should learn he isn't indispensable," she muttered. "Hasn't he ever heard of delegating authority?''

Jane chuckled and gave her a wink. "What that man needs is a wife and a couple of kids to come home to. That would give him the incentive he needs to train a few of his top people to cover for him occasionally. With just him and Sarah alone in that big house, I think he gets lonely.''

Alicia conveyed her opinion of Jane's overzealous imagination with a fulsome snort. Regretting her momentary loss of dignity, she thanked Jane for lunch before leaning forward to kiss her goodbye. But she couldn't resist adding, "The day that man gets lonely for a woman will be the day his prize seed bull gives birth to twins.''

As Alicia drove away, she glanced into the rearview mirror. As she edged out into the street she saw Jane bent over in the middle of the drive, clutching her stomach. Even from this distance Alicia could hear the sound of laughter. "Humph," she muttered indignantly. "I don't see what's so blasted funny.''

Chapter Three

Alicia had debated hard and long, but had finally decided to chance accepting her godmother's invitation to stay with her during the Memorial Day weekend. Sarah had assured her over the phone that Clint wasn't expected home for at least another week, which had eased some of the nervousness she felt whenever she thought about spending three nights under his roof. It wasn't that Sarah wouldn't be an adequate chaperon, it was just that she was blinded by a mother's love and trusted Clint implicitly.

Yet now that Alicia was here, she was very glad she had come. This place held so many wonderful memories for her, she thought with untempered nostalgia. Her parents and godparents had often come here together when she was growing up, the adults to visit with Ben's father while Alicia ran wild over the hills with Clint and Kevin.

The ranch was situated on fifty lush acres set high in the Banner Mountain area of Grass Valley. Although she'd never admit as much to Clint, she, unlike Sarah, loved the peace and isolation of this beautiful spot. With a sigh of pure pleasure she leaned against the wooden porch railing and took a deep breath of the resin-scented air. Her hair tumbled over her slender shoulders as she tilted her head back to fully enjoy the cool breeze.

A rumbling in her stomach attested to the lateness of the hour, but she could hardly complain since it had been her idea to delay dinner. She had arrived about four o'clock and hadn't been able to resist cajoling Sarah into going riding with her. Their love of horses was one of several interests she and her godmother had in common, and Alicia enjoyed nothing better than exploring the many forest trails that were tucked out of sight amidst these gorgeous evergreens.

Alicia glanced over her shoulder, absently rubbing her stomach while she wondered how long it was going to take Sarah to finish preparing for dinner. As she had suspected there was still no sign of her godmother. She had mentioned soaking in a hot bath prior to dressing, and Alicia was well aware of what that meant. Letting her godmother near a bathtub was like dumping a desert-parched duck into a pond. She was almost as bad herself, she admitted honestly, but she'd been too eager to watch the sun descend against this spectacular setting to do more than take a quick shower when they had returned from the stables.

Alicia's eyes softened as she thought of the woman who'd been like a second mother to her. Taller than average, with short brown hair generously peppered with gray, Sarah's features were large boned and well-defined. The fine tracery of wrinkles against her tanned skin was like a road map depicting sensitivity and character. Sarah had a preponderance of both.

She was wise as well as kind, always putting the welfare of those she loved ahead of her own. Alicia's throat tightened with tears as sweetly painful memories overtook her. Sarah and Ben had offered her a home when her parents were killed, but Kevin had insisted that it was better for Alicia if the two of them stayed together. Although she'd been disappointed, Sarah had understood that Kevin needed Alicia to ease his grief as much as Alicia had needed him.

This time of year the evenings were still apt to hold a chill when the sun went down, and Alicia suddenly shivered. Only moon-bathed shadows of the view remained to tantalize her memory and she reluctantly turned to reenter the house. When she reached the living room Sarah was crossing the hallway, her steps brisk against the well-polished hardwood floor.

"I'm sorry I took so long," Sarah apologized sheepishly, "but I couldn't tear myself away from all those delicious bubbles."

"You should be ashamed of yourself," Alicia teased. "I had to go outside to escape the tormenting aroma coming from the kitchen. Am I mistaken, or is that a pot roast I smell?"

"Would I produce less than your favorite meal, you ungrateful child?"

The dinner that followed was every bit as good as Alicia had known it would be, and she envied Sarah her prowess in the kitchen. Her own abilities in that direction were sadly lacking, or at least they were according to Kevin. There must be some truth in her brother's assertions, though, she decided as she helped Sarah with the dishes. The last time she'd invited him and Jane over for dinner the steak was overcooked, the vegetables mushy and the gravy full of lumps. She would have to ask Sarah to give her some pointers while she was here, she resolved with a grin.

"You look like the cat that swallowed the canary," Sarah remarked as they carried their coffee and a slice of deep-dish apple pie into the dining room.

Seating herself, Alicia patted her flat stomach contentedly. "I'm enjoying myself, Sarah. Thank you for inviting me to stay with you this weekend."

To Alicia's surprise, Sarah shifted uneasily and glanced away. "I hope you'll still feel like that when I make a little confession, dear."

Alicia stared at her godmother's strained features in concern. "Hey, it can't be that bad."

She followed her words with a laugh, which was stilled when she noticed Sarah's distracted manner. Then her godmother started to mumble an explanation and Alicia stiffened. Openmouthed, she stared across the table at the other woman in dismay. "What do you mean, Clint might be arriving home ahead of schedule? Just how much ahead of schedule are you talking about?"

Sarah cleared her throat and, although her expression remained placid, her eyes shifted evasively. "Umm, he could arrive home tonight," she whispered.

"Sarah!"

The other woman jumped at the strident sound of her name and sent an appealing glance in Alicia's direction. "How was I to know his business trip would be cut short? I certainly couldn't tell him not to come home when he called this morning to inform me of his change in plans."

Alicia chewed at her lower lip and scowled her displeasure. "You should have let me know."

"If I had you would have canceled your visit."

Alicia narrowed her eyes suspiciously and straightened her back in a semimilitant posture. "Does he know I'm here, Sarah?"

The words the older woman meant to say were deflected by the intensity of Alicia's expression. With a resigned sigh Sarah baldly replied, "Yes, he does."

She hesitated a moment, a puzzled frown pleating her brow before she continued. "Now that I think about it, Clint's behavior seemed quite odd. At first I had the impression he was calling to tell me he'd be away even longer than planned, but when I told him you were visiting he started to laugh."

I'll just bet he did, Alicia thought angrily. "Go on, Sarah. What did he say then?"

"Just that he'd be back sometime this evening and that he was looking forward to a very enjoyable holiday."

"Did he also put it into your head that I'd beg off at the last minute if I knew he was returning?" Alicia asked, fully aware of Clint's devious frame of mind. "Is that why you haven't said anything before now?"

Sarah's hands began to wave wildly in the air and there was bewilderment as well as frustration in her voice as she stammered, "I...I just don't know what's wrong with you children. I swear I don't! All your life you've adored Clinton and he you, but now it seems neither of you can be around each other five minutes without the fur flying.''

''I was rather gullible as a child,'' Alicia replied petulantly. ''In those days I felt honored to be bossed around by your son.''

''Surely Clinton doesn't try to boss you around?'' Sarah asked with amused curiosity.

Alicia stared off into space, a distracted expression in her eyes. ''He certainly tries, for all the good it does him.''

Sarah nodded, her manner contemplative. ''Even as a toddler Clinton knew his own mind.''

Alicia tried to picture Clint as a toddler. The only image that resulted was one of a small boy smashing other children over the head with one of his toys when he didn't get his own way. If his current nature was any example, he'd most likely been a rude, ill-mannered little bully.

Alicia's acrimonious thoughts colored her voice as she said, ''That figures, since he's grown up to be a managing, domineering beast.''

''So was his father,'' Sarah replied with a fond smile.

''I rest my case,'' Alicia muttered.

''But Ben loved me and I had my own way of getting around him.''

''Well, Clint doesn't love me and I don't love him,'' Alicia retorted, staring down at the table so she wouldn't have to look at Sarah as she uttered the half lie. "Anyway, Clint's made of sterner stuff than his father. Getting around him would be like trying to steer a Sherman tank with my pinky."

Sarah sighed and shook her head, her expression pensive. "I wish you and Clinton would work at mending the rift between you, dear. It makes life very difficult for me to have you spitting and clawing at each other all the time. He's my son, but you're the daughter I always wanted. I love you both so much. Can't the two of you try to get along?"

The softly spoken plea brought tears to Alicia's eyes. Her godmother was right to be upset, she admitted guiltily. She'd never considered what their private war was costing Sarah, and only now did Alicia fully realize the unenviable position the older woman was in. Her chest tightened as she remembered all the love and caring she'd been given by Sarah over the years, especially since she'd lost her own mother.

At that moment Sarah looked up from her plate and caught the fleeting anguish in Alicia's expression. Immediately she leaned forward, her voice pleading as she placed a warm hand over Alicia's cold one. "Please don't let Clinton's arrival upset you like this, honey."

Alicia shook her head in a negative gesture. "It isn't that."

"Then what's wrong?" Sarah questioned. "Can't you confide in me?"

"It...it's what you said a-about loving me," she choked out. "I love you, too, but your first loyalty should be to Clint."

"I have more than enough love for both of you," Sarah responded gently.

Alicia was shocked by the fierce surge of protectiveness she felt toward Sarah, and her voice was husky with suppressed emotion when she said, "I just don't want you to be hurt because of me. I...I don't want to come between you and Clint."

Sarah stood up and walked around the table. Then she bent down and put her arms around Alicia, her aged cheek pressed to the red-gold curls. "That will never happen," she whispered assuringly, "because Clinton wouldn't let it. He might roar like a wounded grizzly at times, but a man with his responsibilities is often forced to hide his sensitivity from others. Believe me, he cares too much for you to make you a bone of contention between us."

Her sigh feathered softly against the top of Alicia's bent head. "Clinton has become so accustomed to subduing the man beneath the powerful image he presents to the world that I worry about him, Alicia. He was young to shoulder all the responsibility of Drill Well, and although I urged him to sell out he felt he'd be letting his father down."

Alicia knew this was true, because once in those long-ago days of closeness between them, Clint had confided his feelings to Kevin in her presence. His dreams had always centered around the ranch, not his father's company. It was hard for a man of the land to throw himself into the alien existence of power and high finance, and although Clint had exceeded even Ben's expectations, his heart had never been completely in it.

At least in the beginning it hadn't, she corrected silently. But the wielding of power was an insidious temptation for anyone, and she couldn't help wondering if Clint still held the same values he'd expressed in the past. The thought was painful, and she whispered, "He's changed so much, Sarah."

The other woman nodded and patted Alicia's shoulder. "In the beginning a few unscrupulous individuals tried to take advantage of Clint's youthful inexperience by staging a takeover attempt. They were men his father had trusted —men Clint had known and respected all his life. He fought them and he won, but their betrayal left its mark on him, Alicia. He had to harden himself to survive, but he's really a very gentle, caring man beneath his surface bluster."

Alicia was astounded by the extent of her godmother's maternal delusion, but decided to keep her own counsel. She leaned against Sarah's ample breasts with a naturalness that was a comfort in itself. With a great deal of effort, Alicia forced a laugh. "You'd better make up your mind, Sarah.

There's a big difference between a teddy bear and a grizzly.''

"Is that why you run a mile whenever you see Clinton?'' Sarah teased. "Are you afraid you'll be gobbled up if you get too near to him?''

Sarah's question was too close to Alicia's secret fears and the younger woman shivered. The arms that held her tightened into a hug, yet even as she savored the warmth of the embrace she was unpleasantly conscious of an overpowering sensation of foreboding. Soon she was going to have to meet Clinton Kelly on his home ground and she wasn't exactly overjoyed at the prospect. No, she thought, she wasn't looking forward to it at all.

Chapter Four

Alicia groaned as she swung her feet to the floor and stared into the darkened room with a disgruntled expression on her face. Moonlight glimmered through the large, bow window beside the bed and eerily illuminated her surroundings. Before she could control the urge, a huge yawn emerged from her softly parted lips. With a tired groan of defeat she stretched her lissome body, the inverted tulip shape of the baby-doll pajama top she wore briefly exposing her slender waist.

Her arms slapped against her sides as she lowered them, and she rotated her neck to try to ease the tightness from her shoulder muscles. At the rate she was going she was never going to get to sleep, and with a disgruntled exclamation she reached across the bed to turn on the white-shaded lamp on the nightstand. No matter how hard she tried to shut down her mind, she was nervously aware that Clint could be arriving at any moment.

Experiencing this degree of tension was making her seethe with resentment. She was certain he was only coming home this weekend to bedevil her, and that thought was enough to fan her discontent. In fact for all she knew he'd already arrived. She wouldn't necessarily have heard him, since the road as well as the detached garage was on the opposite side of the house. Yet every time she'd started to doze off she had found herself imagining the sound of an approaching car. Deciding a vivid imagination was the pits, she rubbed the tight muscles in the back of her neck.

She was determined to have a private talk with Clint in the morning. If they were to avoid hurting Sarah they were going to have to reach some kind of understanding. She didn't want her godmother to continue to be upset by their sniping behavior toward each other, which was why she hadn't followed her initial instinct to get out while the getting was good.

Actually pride had strengthened her decision to stay, she admitted reluctantly. She wasn't going to allow herself to be intimidated by a man whose ego was bigger than his brain, and she was damned if she was going to be the cause of disappointing his mother. Sarah had been looking forward to this weekend and Alicia wasn't about to let Mr. Clinton Kelly spoil it for her. Come to that, she wasn't going to let him spoil her own pleasure, either.

Sarah might think of Clint as a cuddly teddy bear, but Alicia had more sense. He had issued a challenge and now he was going to expect her to meet it. The man was as big as a grizzly and twice as dangerous. The thought caused the knot of tension that had formed in her throat to grow to choking proportions. She tried to clear the obstruction and felt like a fool when she jumped at the sound of her own voice.

With another yawn she squinted down at the watch on her wrist and barely managed to hold back a groan. It was after midnight, which was a fact her stomach could confirm. She lowered the hand that cupped her neck and pressed it against her middle, but it was useless to try to suppress her body's reaction to tension. Why was she one of those unfortunate people who became ravenous when they were nervous? she wondered. It was a good thing she hadn't chosen a high-stress career or she'd never be able to find clothes big enough to fit her.

A window-rattling gust of wind jerked Alicia from her thoughts. Tilting her chin with unconscious determination, she crossed the room to search her suitcase for her robe and slippers. She was going to go downstairs and fix a sandwich from the leftover roast, certain that once her hunger was satisfied she'd be able to get to sleep.

Her eyes caught a glimpse of pale gold satin and she dragged it from the bottom of the pile with a triumphant grin that showed the twin dimples in her cheeks. Alicia slipped into the knee-length garment and tied the belt around her waist. Unfortunately for her cold toes, the search for her slippers proved fruitless. As she headed for the door she glanced down at her bare feet with a resigned shrug. She switched on the hall light and started down the curving staircase.

Unfortunately the lights chose that precise instant to go out. The living-room drapes were closed and even the moon failed to illuminate the hallway. Muttering a curse beneath her breath, she searched the shadows with nervous, widening eyes as she groped along the wall with one hand to aid her sense of direction. Sarah kept a flashlight in one of the kitchen drawers, she remembered with relief. All she had to do was reach it and she could check the fuse box in the basement.

Pausing momentarily by the door leading into the kitchen, hopefully she reached for the light switch. When she switched it up and nothing happened she mentally began to scold herself for her childish terror of things that go bump in the night. Childish terror? she questioned with a twinge of amusement.

There wasn't anything childish about that kind of fear but the realization didn't do much to reassure her. She still wouldn't let her foot hang over the side of the bed when she slept because she retained a subconscious certainty that whatever was hiding under there would rise up and eat her toes.

With a pounding heart she shuffled across the cold hardwood floor and slid open the kitchen drawer. She winced as it squeaked eerily, her hand shaking as she reached for the flashlight. The moon glow coming through the window over the sink didn't help reduce her fears one iota; if anything the wavering reflections it cast against the pine cabinets worsened her trepidation.

Alicia pressed the button on the flashlight and nothing happened. With a great deal of agitation she scrambled through the drawer in search of fresh batteries, wanting to howl with disappointment when none magically appeared at her fingertips. There was no way she was going down into that dark basement without being able to see her hand in front of her face, she decided, but just then she felt a thick candle stub.

With a relieved exclamation she grabbed it and headed for the gas-operated stove. As flame ate greedily at the wick she relaxed a little and turned toward the entrance to the basement. Edging through the opening with one hand lifted to protect her only source of light, she let out a frightened yelp as the door slammed shut behind her. She started down the steep stairs, grimacing in distaste as the soles of her feet collected gritty sediment from the freezing cement surface.

Although it provided some visibility, to her dismay the candle also shed terrifying images on the roughly hewn walls. By the time she reached the bottom of the stairs Alicia was in a cold sweat. As she turned she kept her eyes fixed resolutely on the flickering flame, but her attention was so concentrated that at first she didn't notice one of the shadows detaching itself from the far wall. When she did, she let out a piercing scream. The candle went out, dropping from her nerveless fingers as Alicia stumbled backward in the pitch blackness. Unfortunately there was some kind of obstruction in her path that caught the back of her knees and sent her flying. The breath left her lungs in a loud whoosh and her bottom met the basement floor with a painful thump. It was then she heard it—the low, sibilant hiss of laughter that raised havoc with every hair follicle on her body.

"Who...who's there?"

Alicia's frantic question was greeted by a sepulchral chuckle, which sounded even more sinister than before. Oh, God! she thought frantically as her ears became attuned to a shuffling noise. Whoever or whatever was down here with her was coming closer, and she was reminded of a late movie she'd once seen on television. She had watched the film as intently as she could, staring through the splayed fingers of her hands covering her face as the floor of an old farmhouse burst upward in a fiery mass. She vividly recalled her horror as a creature from hell reached out and dragged the screaming heroine into the raging inferno. Even a knowledge of self-defense wouldn't have helped the poor woman then, she'd realized with a shudder.

It was definitely the wrong memory to have at this particular moment, and Alicia cowered instinctively while rapidly scooting backward across the gritty cement. If the floor opened up, she decided with hysterical cowardice, she would be damned if she was going to be close enough to whatever was underneath it to be grabbed.

Just then a towering specter loomed in front of her and she felt her shoulders clamped in an unbreakable grip. Knowing only a hideous demon could possess such supernatural strength, she acted on pure gut instinct. Opening her mouth, she let loose a screech fit to wake the dead. Much to her amazement she was immediately released, which encouraged her to keep on screaming.

"Oh, my God, don't do that!"

The cry was decidedly masculine and thoroughly overpowered her own voice. Startled by the human sound Alicia stopped wailing but forgot to close her mouth. When sudden light flooded her dank, dingy surroundings she jerked her head back to get a good look at her tormentor. Unfortunately she'd misjudged exactly where on the dank cement she was sitting. Two things happened simultaneously. The sharp movement of her head brought the back of her skull into abrupt and painful contact with the wall, and she recognized Clint.

Alicia quickly let go with another howl, this time one of pure rage. "You fiend," she intoned hoarsely. "You callous, insensitive brute!"

She gained great satisfaction from his reaction. In a synchronized movement his hand left the electrical panel he was leaning against and grabbed at his chest. Then his entire body slumped against the wall and he uttered a particularly virulent curse. "I asked you not to do that, woman! Are you trying to give me a heart attack?"

"Isn't that what you were trying to do to me, sneaking around down here?"

"I was changing a fuse."

"Oh," she drawled sarcastically. "Is that why you didn't answer me when I called out? Odd, I never heard of anyone changing fuses with their teeth."

"Don't be flippant, Angel," he said on a deeply drawn breath. "After the fright you gave me I think we're even."

"We'll never be even, Clinton Benjamin Kelly!" She remained on the floor against the rough wall, shaking now from temper instead of fright. "You're going to pay for this if it takes me till my dying day."

A wide grin split his mobile mouth and his eyes danced wickedly as he looked down at her, surveying her disheveled state. "I just wanted to prove you're not as brave and invincible as you think you are."

Alicia started to tell him to go to hell, but when she looked up at him her attention was caught by that smile. He looked damnably attractive, his dark hair ruffled, his black shirt open nearly to his wide leather belt. Her gaze drifted lower, and she was suddenly painfully embarrassed by the full extent of her feminine curiosity. For goodness sake, Alicia, she reprimanded herself sharply, this is no time to give your imagination a clear field!

For lack of a more appropriate distraction she focused her attention on her dust-covered feet, stretched out in front of her. Yet to her everlasting shame, her mind burned with his image. Physically she was conscious of him in every particle of her body, and her toes curled in reaction. Her breathing had almost slowed to normal, but now it was accelerating again to an alarming degree.

Just when she became aware of his fixed gaze on the front of her robe she couldn't have said. Maybe it was more an instinct than actually noticing where he was looking, because by the time she saw that her robe was gaping, her breasts were already tingling.

With a gasp she drew the edges of the fabric together, hectic color rising in her cheeks as she absorbed his interest in the scantiness of her attire.

Alicia's lips pursed in annoyance. "Will you stop?"

One dark eyebrow lifted quizzically and his features assumed an air of bland innocence that made her want to slap him. "Stop what?"

"Stop looking at me like that."

"How am I looking at you?" His thigh muscles bulged as he knelt in front of her. That impressive indication of his masculinity combined with his husky drawl made her swallow heavily. She thought her lungs would burst as she held her breath and defensively drew her knees to her chest. The tremulous look she shot him complemented her sudden inability to answer. Alicia was way out of her league and no one knew it better than she.

One long, gentle finger reached out to tilt up her chin. The movement of his arm caused the edges of his shirt to part more fully and she shivered convulsively at the sensual promise in his gleaming black eyes. She wasn't sure if she was more afraid of him or of herself in that instant. She had the strongest urge to throw herself against his hard body and rub her heated cheeks over the dark hair on his bronzed chest. Her lips quivered with the longing to press against the dark male nipple she could see peeking through that luxuriant covering.

Clint's finger slid slowly downward until it pressed against the pulse pounding visibly in her throat. She bit down hard on her lower lip to stop its trembling and tried to move away from the taunting touch. "Don't," she whispered.

"Don't want you?" he asked hoarsely. "That will take some doing to accomplish, Angel."

"At least stop calling me that," she cried, mustering all her willpower to resist the spell he was weaving around her. "I'm not an angel."

With a strength she envied he drew her to her feet. "Aren't you?" he questioned softly. "You look like one with those big gray eyes and your soft silky skin. Do you know how badly I want to touch you, Alicia?"

"Clint, please..."

"I can make you lose that angel innocence," he murmured, "and cause those haunting eyes of yours to glow with a pleasure you haven't even begun to imagine."

"I...I didn't want you to come home this weekend." Alicia immediately wanted to take back her words, inwardly wincing at how defensive they sounded.

"Didn't you realize I'd return as soon as I found out you were going to be here?"

The amusement in his voice aided her determination to resist his seduction. "No, I didn't."

"You mean my mother didn't mention my arrival to you?"

She frowned with discomfiture. "Well, yes, but not until dinner tonight."

He gave her a mocking smile. "You still had ample opportunity to run like a frightened rabbit."

"I'm not a petrified bunny." Her defiant exclamation ended in a squeal when he bent down and lifted her into his arms. "What are you doing?"

"I'm going to teach you not to be afraid of me."

"As I just said," she exclaimed haughtily, "I am not in the least intimidated by you, Mr. Kelly."

He clicked his tongue in reproof. "Angels should never tell lies."

She punched his shoulder with a curled fist, frustrated when the blow had absolutely no effect on him. "Put me down this instant, Clint."

"Not until I teach you a few home truths, darling."

Clint climbed the stairs with a speed that alarmed her. She peeked at him through her lashes and the expression on his face nearly stopped her heart. There was implacable determination stamped on his compressed mouth, and the look in his eyes made her squirm in a panicky attempt to be free.

"Stop wriggling," he commanded abruptly, "or we're both going to land in a heap at the bottom of these stairs."

Alicia gritted her teeth. "Then put me down, damn you!"

Clint's low tones mocked her demand. "All in good time."

They entered the kitchen and Alicia glared at the brightly burning lights. Where were you when I needed you? she thought petulantly. Channeling some of her resentment into her voice, she repeated her demand. "Put me down this instant, Clinton!"

With a low laugh he did as she asked, but not in the way she expected. Instead he plunked her onto the kitchen counter, and she yelped when her rear made contact with the hard, mosaic tile. "That hurt," she protested.

"Is your bottom sore from scooting around the basement floor?"

Alicia stiffened and remarked with ghoulish precision, "I . . . am going . . . to murder you."

"Not until I've washed your feet," he uttered calmly. "I don't want you getting the sheets dirty."

Alicia stared at him and wondered just whose sheets he was referring to. The suspicion barely entered her mind before she was hurling her body toward the floor. Clint's lips curved with irritating complacency as his large hand easily prevented her escape. The breath pushed out of her lungs as the heat from his palm penetrated her clothing to her stomach; the resultant ache of desire she felt shocked her into silence.

"Don't tell me you're finally through fighting me."

Alicia clamped her lips together, stubbornness in every rigid angle of her body as he wet a washrag and gently began bathing her feet. She would never stop fighting to keep her freedom from this man, she vowed silently. To surrender would be to lose her independence and the ability to be a person in her own right. He would demand everything she had to give—her soul as well as her body.

Clint wouldn't understand her need for equality in their relationship because he was used to controlling everything in his life. She couldn't let him control her, she resolved with a combination of fear and anguish. Even though it meant fighting her own love for him, somehow she had to escape the cage she felt closing around her.

Chapter Five

Alicia experienced a weak, giddy sensation as Clint continued to carefully wipe the grime from her feet. She became fascinated by the slow movements of his hands. They were strong yet gentle and she didn't want to think of the pleasure she was deriving from his touch. To do so would be insanity, she realized, and would leave her with no defense against his blatant sexuality.

By the time Clint was finished, Alicia's closed fists were pressed against her sides and her eyes were closed. She heard the plop of the wet cloth as it hit the sink but still she refused to look at him. Then there was the whisper of warm breath against her face and her lashes moved in a startled flutter as she felt a sliding caress against the hollow of her throat.

Alicia's eyes shot open as heat coursed through her, but no matter how blissful the sensation she couldn't allow this intimacy to continue. The upper folds of her robe were gaping open again and Clint's gaze was on the brief top of her baby-doll pajamas. Although the thin, cotton fabric was modest enough, from the look on his face the man had X-ray vision.

Well, she decided angrily, she wasn't going to let him go on thinking she enjoyed being inspected like one of his prime head of beef. Firming her mouth into a mutinous slant, she glared up at him. "If that knuckle wanders any lower I'll break your arm."

Clint laughed out loud and she resented the tingle of response she felt at the sound. She resented even more the hand that wrapped around the hair at her nape, but before she could protest his proprietary touch he whispered, "You remind me of a banty hen, all ruffled feathers and pecking beak. Aren't you a trifle small for such a threat?"

Even though she knew he was only trying to get a rise out of her, Alicia's eyes flashed with indignation. "Try me and see."

Another chuckle emerged, this one deeper and more disturbing than the last. "I think I will," he agreed with a wicked gleam in his eyes.

Her own gaze followed the source of the engaging sound, tracing the shape of his lips. Lord, but he has a beautiful mouth, she thought as she became enamored with each indentation and full, inviting curve. "Will what?" she asked with a distracted air.

"Try you."

His innuendo was so inviting she almost croaked "All right" before she stopped herself. Gooseflesh popped out all over her body at the near miss. Thoroughly annoyed by her weak-kneed reaction, she retorted, "You're underestimating me, Clint. Don't make the mistake of thinking I'll just calmly sit here and let you play with me. When I want a lover I'll ask for one."

"You know I'd never deny you anything you want."

The exclamation was shiveringly soft and oh, so promising. I'll just bet you wouldn't, she thought with a faltering attempt at derision, as she paused momentarily to think of all the wondrous, sexy things she did want him to try. But it was an exercise in futility and she ground her teeth as she struggled against the insane urge to throw herself into his arms. "In case you've forgotten, I've been trained to take care of myself. Just because we're practically related, don't imagine I'll hesitate to use my skills on you."

"There's no blood tie between us," he reminded her with obvious satisfaction, "and I'd much rather imagine you with this beautiful hair spread across my pillow."

Alicia's mouth went dry at the picture his words created in her mind. Her voice cracked slightly but she maintained her defiant attitude. "Will you please take me seriously for one blasted second?"

His gaze locked with hers. "Believe me I am taking you seriously, Alicia. You're the one who needs to readjust your thinking."

"I don't know why you should say that, Clint."

She stared at him in exasperation. If her thinking got anymore adjusted, she thought wryly, she'd be melded to his lean body in an instant. Thankfully he didn't yet fully realize that where he was concerned her common sense was as dead as the dodo. For the better part of her life she'd ached to have this man look at her the way he was now doing, and she was only just discovering that desire alone wasn't enough to satisfy her.

Alicia knew she had to be respected for the woman she was, not viewed as a plaything for his delectation or as a convenient hostess for his home. She wanted to be needed, to be as necessary to his survival as the breath he drew into his lungs. She wanted to be the sun in his sky as he was in hers. Considering the fluctuating state of her emotions, she was proud of the firmness in her voice when she remarked, "My mind is perfectly clear on this subject. I won't be seduced or badgered into marriage."

"You can seduce me if you'd prefer," he replied with maddening indulgence.

The laugh that bubbled up from her chest caught her completely unaware, and with an aggrieved shake of her head she gurgled, "You idiot."

His teeth flashed in a winsome smile. "Why don't you call me 'darling' instead?"

The appellation held too much appeal, and she tilted her chin imperiously. "What I call you makes little difference."

"It does to me," he remarked lazily. "I refuse to be seduced by a woman who refers to me as an idiot."

"I am not going to seduce you," she ground out tightly, no longer finding any humor in their conversation.

"Why?" he drawled softly. "You're ready for me now."

"Oh, no I'm not," she said on a gulp, edging backward when he shifted closer to her. The taut angle of her jaw, which spoke of both pride and stubbornness, only seemed to deepen his certainty that she was his for the taking. To her dismay his patent lack of belief in her denial didn't make her as angry as she thought it should. His knowledgeable grin was enchanting and she wanted to press the tip of her finger to the full curve of his lower lip so badly that she shivered with the effort it took to keep herself from reaching out to him.

Clint saw the telltale quiver and his own body tensed. "I think you're more than ready for me," he uttered hoarsely.

Alicia just stared at him. She couldn't have denied his assertion if her life had depended on it. To do so she would have had to utter another lie, but the way he was looking at her demanded truth between them. He was no longer smiling and his eyes had darkened with an abundance of turbulent emotion that caught at her breath. The hunger in his smoldering gaze was a revelation, and she was too weak with her own longing to resist when he grasped her waist and pulled her forward.

She was balanced precariously on the edge of the counter, but in a sudden maneuver that drew a choked groan from her throat, Clint moved between her thighs. "Wrap you legs around me," he urged in strangled tones.

"No, I . . ."

"God, you're driving me out of my mind," he moaned, taking the initiative and guiding her legs until they formed a tight circle around his lean, muscular hips.

Clint pushed her robe aside, and his mobile fingers slid over her thighs. For a brief heart-stopping moment he caressed her bare flesh, then his hands quickly continued their journey until he was grasping her buttocks. He lifted her more fully and with a gasp he pressed against her. Then he lowered his head and his mouth blindly sought her own. His kiss was open and hot and so sweet she wanted to die with the taste and texture of his probing tongue. His fingers squeezed her tightening flesh and his body matched the rhythm, leaving her in no doubt as to the rigid completeness of his arousal.

Alicia felt dizzy and she grabbed at his shoulders to stop the room from spinning. Immediately she was pressed even closer to his hard male flesh and she arched her back in mindless acceptance of the intimacy he had initiated between them. Her body softened and yielded with melting fervency until she thought she would scream with the pleasure he was giving her.

Instead she uttered a choked sob, and when Clint stiffened, her fingers slid in silent demand across his shoulders. She gripped his neck, her nails digging into his skin to leave her mark on him. The rapid thud of his heart struck against her breasts, which felt full and aching with a sensitivity she'd never experienced. Alicia was out of control in a way she hadn't known was possible; her only desire was to hold him as tightly as she could until the tremors quaking through her eased.

With a muffled groan he tore his mouth from hers and said soothingly, "Easy, baby. Let me help you come down slow and easy."

Clint began to rub her back in sweeping strokes, while he feathered tender kisses against her flushed cheeks. "I...I didn't realize," she cried incredulously. "I..."

He was breathing as unsteadily as she was, and with a final shudder he buried his mouth against her tangled hair. "So now you know what I want from you, Angel."

Alicia stared across the room, her eyes glazed with the lingering remnants of passion. Yes, she thought incredulously as she lowered her head to his shoulder and held on to him for the support she so badly needed. Yes, now she knew what he expected from her. It was like dying and being reborn and she was more certain than ever that she would be lost to herself if she gave him that kind of control over her. Her love for him made her weak and it was a weakness that held a high price. A price, she thought sadly, that she could never afford to pay if she valued her own self-respect.

As though of its own volition her open mouth found the pulsing cord in his strong neck, and she whispered, "You want too much."

Clint arched his throat and moaned with sensual enjoyment. "Mmm, that's nice."

"You're not listening," she protested shakily.

"That's one of my worst failings."

"I meant it, Clint," she reaffirmed, barely resisting the temptation to nibble at his ear. Pulling her head back, she sighed in frustration. "You're a very possessive man."

He nodded, his features as serious as her own. "Where you're concerned I'm practically manic."

"That's why I can't marry you," she countered bitterly. "At first I thought you proposed because you couldn't satisfy your desire for me without causing insurmountable problems with our families. That wasn't the only reason, was it?"

"No," he bit out tersely.

For what seemed an eternity she waited for him to explain away her suspicions. Alicia listened for words like love and need, desperately wanting to be told that he, too, felt this burning desire to be made whole. She waited in vain, his silence in itself a condemnation. Suddenly she felt tired and disillusioned and hurting in a way that demanded an outlet.

Alicia found her release in a sarcasm that made her inwardly recoil from the stridency of her own voice. "No, I'm just convenient, aren't I? You've decided it's time you had a wife, and with the ruthless logic you apply to everything else, you decided I was the most likely candidate."

She drew in a deep breath to regain some control over her emotions. Her eyes closed for an instant, and when they opened she looked at him with a disdain that hid the emptiness in her heart. "It's such a tidy solution and so pitilessly cold-blooded, Clint. I'm the sister of your best friend and you know me well enough to be certain I'm not after your fortune. Add to that the fact that your mother already loves me like a daughter, and you have instant cooperation on all fronts."

His expression had grown distant, his eyes as rigidly implacable as twin pieces of jet. There was a cynical edge to his voice when he muttered, "You seem to have formed your own conclusions, Alicia. It would be a wasted effort on my part to try to change your mind."

There was a tightness building in her chest that was so painful she wanted to cry out, but instead she managed to say calmly, "I can't marry you just because it's convenient, especially when you've demonstrated your intention to dominate me through sheer force of will, Clint. You want a piece of paper that gives you the right to take over my life, but I won't be owned by any man. I went from the care of my parents to being looked after by Kevin, and now you want me to simply yield my hard won independence to you. Well, I won't do it."

"Don't talk like a fool," he grated harshly, all his earlier gentleness disappearing in a flash of his smoldering eyes. "All this drivel about independence is just a smoke screen for you to hide behind, Alicia."

"Can't or won't, it doesn't really matter," she replied listlessly.

"Do you want me to crawl?" he demanded. "Will that satisfy the perverse streak in your nature? Will it make you feel more independent to humble me? If it will convince you that I don't intend to treat you like some damned windup toy, then to hell with my pride!"

"You don't understand me at all, do you?" she questioned, her eyes filling with tears. "You speak with scorn of my need to keep my independence, because you have no real respect for me."

Clint shook his head, unmoved by the sadness in her voice. "I understand you better than you do yourself," he remarked coldly. "Isn't it about time you stopped competing with the boys and let yourself be a woman?"

Alicia gasped and pushed against his chest with all her strength. "Why? So you can use your sexual skill to keep me in my place?" she snapped. "You'd like that, wouldn't you, Clint? What better weapon to use against me than my desire for you. But you're not going to get the chance. When I marry it will be to a man who views me as his equal, and I'll never settle for anything less."

If he hadn't chosen to step aside she wouldn't have been able to budge him, but to her relief Clint let her slide to the floor. But he remained in front of her, blocking any attempt she might make to leave. "Will you let me pass, please?"

"Not until you listen to some sense," he said with restrained violence. "I want you to open that closed little mind of yours and hear what I have to say for a change."

She pursed her lips in annoyance but didn't react to the insult. "I'm listening."

"First of all I do not use sex as a weapon. Secondly I do not view you as some kind of inferior being."

She sniffed disdainfully and fixed him with a disbelieving gaze. Instantly his arm snaked around her waist and he pulled her against him with grim-faced determination. "All right," he gritted harshly. "So don't believe me. But at least you've finally admitted you want me. I suppose it's a step in the right direction."

"Not for me, it isn't."

The childish petulance in her voice seemed to dispel Clint's anger. The smile he gave her was slow and sweet and held a depth of knowledge that dismayed her. He brushed a few strands of hair from her flushed cheek with a tenderness that completely destroyed her determination to resist him. "My little firebrand," he sighed impatiently. "What am I going to do with you?"

"Leave me alone?" she asked hopefully.

"You don't really want that and you know it."

With a breathlessness she deplored she managed to wedge her arms between them, but even that barrier couldn't erase the thrill that burned along her nerve ends. She was shaken by the extent of her lingering desire, her nipples pebble hard where they had been pressed against his chest. No, she realized with a sense of hopelessness, she didn't want him to leave her alone. Her mouth might speak the lies but her body knew the truth only too well.

Alicia lowered her lashes to avoid the knowing expression that added a new depth to his black eyes. Determined to hide her weakness from him, she admitted, "I respond to you physically, but in all the ways that matter you're wrong for me, Clint."

He tapped the end of her nose and her eyes flew open. Then he cupped her chin and tilted her head back until she couldn't avoid looking at him. "We do have quite a problem, don't we?"

She frowned, her expression puzzled. "Isn't that what I've been telling you?"

"You've been telling me what you want in a relationship—not how you expect to get it."

"I don't understand."

"We're a pretty potent combination physically. Do you agree?"

She flushed and her head jerked in an assenting nod. "Yes," she whispered with a defeated grimace. "After what just happened between us it wouldn't do me any good to deny it."

Clint's face softened with approval as he searched her eyes. "Then the way I see it," he murmured quietly, "the most obvious difficulty we have to overcome is ignorance."

She stared at him in surprise. "What do you mean?"

"I think our real problem is that we don't know each other well enough," he said firmly.

"Clint, I've known you all my life."

He shook his head, the negative movement quietly assured. "We may have spent a lot of time together over the years, but we've formed a lot of misconceptions along the way. We need to make a new start."

Alicia couldn't doubt his sincerity, but she did doubt the feasibility of what he was suggesting. She dug her teeth into her bottom lip and gnawed indecisively. "How can we do that after all this time?"

"By spending as many waking hours together as possible."

Just the thought caused Alicia to tense. How could she be with Clint and not give herself away? she wondered frantically. She could withstand his seduction from a distance but the prospect of being with him on a regular basis was more than she could bear. With a violent shake of her head she muttered, "I don't think that's an acceptable solution for either of us, Clint."

"Haven't you ever heard of compromise, Alicia?"

"With you any compromising would be done by me."

"You don't trust me at all, do you?"

"I can't afford to," she stated coolly. "Now if you don't mind I'd like to go to bed."

He tightened his hold until she was plastered against him from her collarbone to her quaking knees. "Then tell me," he asked silkily, "what are we going to do about our desire for each other?"

She gulped audibly and fixed her gaze somewhere around the middle of his chest. "Put a lid on it?"

His big body began to shake with laughter. "We'll play it your way for now," he agreed in a soft growl, "but don't be misled, Angel. Someday soon that lid is going to blow sky high and when it does you're going to have to accept the consequences."

Clint released her suddenly and she scurried for safety without worrying about maintaining her dignity. The door made a slight swishing sound as it closed behind her, but she was still able to hear the cryptic note in his voice when he muttered, "I only hope I can go the distance, Angel."

Chapter Six

The coal-black horses galloped up a steep incline, Alicia and Clint hunched low over their straining necks. The sound of hooves pounding against the bracken-strewn path rang loudly in the stillness of approaching dusk, with Clint and Alicia's laughter the only accompaniment to the surging sound. The thick woods that covered the path opened up at the top of the hill and at the last possible moment one horse drew ahead. Reining his horse with difficulty, Clint noticed the disgruntled expression on Alicia's face as her horse surged up and passed his.

Struggling to leash the excited power of her mount, Alicia gradually halted the magnificent beast's progress and returned to where Clint was smugly waiting. "You cheated," she accused with a grin.

His brows lifted in an inquiring arc. "How do you figure that?"

"You didn't give me enough of a head start and you know very well that Sundown can't match Caliph for speed."

Clint leaned forward to pat the neck of his stallion, giving Alicia a sidelong glance as he did so. "I counted to twenty but Caliph is like me, honey. He's not likely to let that mare of yours get away from him."

Alicia gave an exaggerated sigh as Caliph snuffled Sundown's heaving flank. Alicia fluttered her eyelashes at Clint. "They're in love."

Giving a shout of laughter, Clint's eyes danced wickedly. "So are we."

At his words Alicia's eyes darkened with uneasiness, her heart pounding from more than a recent exertion. During the past two days Clint had been treating her with the easy familiarity of a friend, so his verbal love play now was disturbing. When Sundown shied away from Caliph, Alicia tightened her knees and drew back on the reins. She could understand the mare's nervousness at being crowded by the big stallion since she felt much same way about Caliph's rider.

Evidently reacting to the confusion he saw in Alicia's expression, Clint pulled his gaze from her face.

His broad chest expanded as he drew a deep breath of the pungently scented air into his lungs. He made a sweeping gesture with his arm. "Look at that sunset, Angel. Have you ever seen anything more beautiful?"

Distracted from her intense awareness of the disturbing man beside her, Alicia looked around her. From their vantage point the green and verdant valley was spread out like a picture postcard for their delectation. The view before her was perfect, and her smoky eyes glowed with appreciation. Below them spread a grassy meadow intersected by pristine white fences, gnarled-limbed oak trees, tall ponderosa pines and Douglas firs. An indigo sky added the final touch to nature's colorful palate, as the kiss of the dying day began to fade through dark blue into black.

The sun hadn't completely set, yet the moon was already visible. Certain evenings in the foothill country of the Sierra Nevadas were like that, she mused, with the sun, moon and stars so close together at times that it seemed as though the angels could leap from one fairy-dusted surface to another. The fanciful imagery flitting through her mind made her mouth tilt with wry awareness of her own romanticism.

As she glanced at Clint, her voice was hushed and husky with emotion. "Is there any place on earth as lovely as this?"

"I don't think so," he replied quietly, his gaze fixed on the distant horizon. "I've seen beautiful country when I've gone away on business but I always hunger for the sight of home."

"I wouldn't mind traveling but I don't think I could be happy living anywhere else."

Clint glanced toward her and smiled his understanding. "Your roots are here."

His simple statement made her feel linked to him by an invisible force. Her mother and father had moved to Grass Valley shortly after their marriage, yet she wondered how much stronger her feelings toward this country might be if she shared Clint's background. This land had been in his family for over three generations; the Kellys were direct descendants of the early pioneers who had come seeking gold and stayed to found the town.

Clint's eyes were once again searching the horizon, his features relaxed and thoughtful. "I've never understood how my father could have preferred town life to living on the ranch," he remarked softly. "He grew up here but he was a businessman to his fingertips. I feel obligated to continue the business he founded, but I take after my grandfather in my love of the land."

Alicia remembered Clint's grandfather with a great deal of fondness. Old Abel Kelly had been an irascible gentleman who had imbued his grandson with the feelings for his inheritance that his son didn't share. Clint had spent a great deal of time with Abel while growing up, as had she and Kevin. So many years had passed since those faraway days, yet when she visited the ranch she always experienced a sense of security and belonging that she didn't feel anywhere else.

"This land casts a timeless spell," she whispered dreamily. "The world is constantly changing, but these hills and trees were here before we were born and will remain long after we're gone."

"Do you find that thought comforting, Alicia?"

"Yes," she responded on a sigh. "I know progress is necessary, but once all of Grass Valley was this open and free, Clint. I think it would kill something in my soul to have developers strip away all of this beauty to build more houses and offices. There's so little unspoiled country left for us to enjoy."

Tenderly he ran his hand over her shining curls, his eyes piercing her defenses with a single glance. "You're like this land, honey. There is so much unspoiled loveliness inside of you waiting for the right man to share it with. You make me ache with longing, Angel."

He drew his hand away, but his imprint still burned against her flesh. Alicia's breath caught in her throat as she looked at him. He sat straight and proud in the saddle, his profile silhouetted by the fading sun. He seemed assured and indomitable, yet oddly vulnerable. Suddenly she wanted to reach out and return his touch. The need shocked her and with restless nervousness she dismounted to distance herself from him. He was too close, too overpowering for her to retain her peace of mind. Even though he was keeping his physical demands in check, his emotional assault on her senses was stronger than ever.

The creak of leather told her that Clint was descending from Caliph's back, and she mentally steeled herself as he drew up beside her. "Clint, please don't pressure me, I . . ."

"Then don't run from me," he pleaded gently, his arm encircling her shoulders as he turned her to face him. "There's no place to go, Alicia."

With a broken murmur she lowered her head to his chest and trembled when his arms tightened around her. "No," she agreed quietly. "There's no place to go."

Alicia bit into a peanut-butter-and-jelly sandwich, her head bent over the pile of applications Kevin had left on her desk. According to his note he wanted two positions for security guards filled yesterday—a pressure she certainly hadn't needed this morning. She'd arrived home from her long weekend at the ranch late Monday afternoon, yet today was Friday and she still hadn't caught up with the backlog that had greeted her return.

Lord, but she was tired. She hadn't slept properly for so long she felt like a hag. Work should have proved a distraction, but lack of proper rest was making her irritable and unable to concentrate. She was also eating like a pig, she thought glumly as she stared with distaste at the sandwich in her hand.

She didn't have to look far for the reason. Thoughts of Clint were driving her bonkers, she decided with disgusted certainty. Their days together at the ranch had made the barriers she'd erected between them seem as insubstantial as the blush of a dawn mist. Her contentment with him had touched her in a new, unexpected way...a way as seductive and beguiling as anything that had gone before. He had reverted in some mystical manner to the old Clint, a young man with dreams and trust visible in his beautiful dark eyes.

This constant battle she was fighting with herself dismayed her. Were those brief glimpses of him last weekend permitting her an insight into the real man behind the facade that Sarah had alluded to, or was he merely putting on a new hat to gain her confidence? Once she had given in to him, would he again become domineering and unresponsive to her needs? Would he help her to grow as an individual as the years passed or deprive her of her independence and self-respect? Would he let her share his life or push her into the background? She still hadn't found the answers to those questions, and her uncertainty was making it nearly impossible for her to get through the days . . . and the nights.

The bit of sandwich she'd been chewing for the better part of five minutes stuck in her throat like glue, and Alicia took a small sip from the milk she'd taken out of the aged-but-working refrigerator they kept in the employees' lounge. Frowning down at the small, inoffensive carton as though its offerings were rancid, she mumbled an expletive and wrapped up the rest of her lunch. Getting slowly to her feet, she returned both the wrinkled paper sack and the milk carton to the fridge before going back to her office.

It wasn't any wonder that her appetite was off, she thought as she entered the windowless room. She had been stuffing herself with junk food all morning and enough was enough! Plopping down in her leather chair, she propelled it from side to side with her feet. As it squeaked and swiveled her irritation increased, as did the doubts she was having about Clint.

During her stay at the ranch she'd often felt as though she were living with Dr. Jekyll while waiting for Mr. Hyde to appear. All the fresh, country air she'd drawn into her lungs hadn't prevented her from tossing and turning at night. Just knowing Clint was only a short distance away from her had kept her mind awake and her body tense. She had yearned to have him beside her in bed, his hands and mouth teaching her all the things she yearned to know.

Alicia had hoped the torment would stop once she was back home, but her apartment hadn't been the refuge she'd needed. Over the past few days her desire for Clint had increased until she wondered if she would ever stop aching, and there was nowhere she could go to escape his shadow. Whenever she thought about him she grew hot one moment and cold the next. Sweet heaven, she missed him so much she despaired of her ability to withstand the appeal just picturing his face in her mind could cause. She wanted to be with him, and what scared her most was the realization that she was coming closer and closer to giving him what he wanted without counting the cost to herself.

Absentmindedly she picked up a cookie from the package open on her desk but stopped herself before she could get it into her mouth. Staring at it in disgust, she arched her hand over her head and the sweet landed with a ringing thud in the metal wastebasket in the corner. The unusual method of disposal reminded Alicia of the many hours she had spent with her brother and Clint beneath the basketball hoop that had been attached to their garage when she was a child. The tight line of her mouth softened when she remembered Clint's patience as he'd taught her the rudiments of the game. So much of her life had been centered around him. She signed resignedly.

"Alicia, I've got to talk to you," a voice demanded from the doorway.

Startled, Alicia motioned Sarah into the room with a pleased smile. But the smile faded when she noticed the lace handkerchief the older woman was twisting between her fingers. "What is it, Sarah?" she asked uneasily. "What's wrong?"

In strangled accents her godmother uttered a single name. "Clinton."

Alicia thought she might never breathe again as she rose slowly to her feet. Had something happened to Clint? With a feeling of faintness she remembered that he'd been due to fly back home this morning. With an indistinguishable whimper she pressed both palms against her desk and leaned forward, her gaze fixed on Sarah's distraught features as she whispered tormentedly, "The plane... It didn't...?"

Sarah seemed puzzled for an instant, then horrified realization drained the color from her face. Lifting her hand in a gesture of remorse, she rushed forward to wrap her arms around Alicia's trembling frame. "Oh, darling, I'm so sorry. I never thought you'd think... Of course the plane didn't crash. Dear God, me and my idiotic dramatics. Clinton is fine, Alicia. He arrived home this morning safe and sound."

Alicia's face crumpled as she dropped into her chair, Sarah's arms not strong enough to hold her upright. Resting her elbows on the edge of her desk, Alicia leaned forward to cup her head in her hands. Dots of light flickered behind the blackness of her closed eyelids as her mind withdrew into the past. She could visualize the newspaper she'd retrieved from the fireplace, remember the pictures of pieces of wreckage spread for half a mile over a snow-encrusted mountain.

Tears flowed past her splayed fingers as she recalled how wild Clint had been when he had found her cowering in the big chair in his study, her eyes sightless as she stared down at the mangled paper in her hand. He had tried to protect her from the more grisly aspects of her parents' death, but she'd had to know. He had lifted her from his chair and sat down with her in his lap, holding her until some of his warmth had penetrated her shivering flesh.

The sound of his voice had soothed the anguished rigidity from her body, and for the first time since the accident had occurred she'd given way to her grief. His fingers had feathered gently through her hair, his tender voice urging her to let go of the pain. She had fallen asleep like a baby in his arms. For three days she had roused herself only long enough for him to carry her to the bathroom or coax her to eat.

Not once had he left her side, she remembered with a muffled sob. When Kevin arrived for the funeral from the army base where he was stationed, Clint was haggard and red eyed from lack of sleep, his movements stiff and uncoordinated as he lifted himself from the chair beside her bed to greet his friend. He hadn't let anyone else near her, not even his mother.

Clint...oh, Clint! At last she accepted the full depth of her feelings for him. He was arrogant, dictatorial, stubborn, impossible...and she loved him with every atom of her being. They might never have a future together as man and wife, but she wouldn't want to exist in a world without him in it. Just the thought was unbearable!

"Alicia, don't tremble so," Sarah urged, her voice filled with tears. "Please, darling...please don't do this to yourself. I'm so sorry, so very sorry for barging in here like a blundering old fool."

Alicia knuckled the moisture from her ashen cheeks like a child, and tried to smile reassuringly at Sarah, but her lips still trembled. "It's all right," she muttered hollowly. "It was my fault for jumping to conclusions."

Clicking her tongue, Sarah bustled from the office and returned with a glass of water. Alicia gave her a weak nod as she accepted the offering, which was Sarah's usual panacea. But as she took a sip and cautiously swallowed past the tightness in her throat, Alicia raised her head to look at her godmother. The grooved lines beside Sarah's compressed lips reminded Alicia that something was still dreadfully wrong.

Her hand was shaking so badly the liquid sloshed over the rim of the glass. With exaggerated care she put her drink down on the green felt blotter in front of her. "What's happened, Sarah?"

Stiffening her spine, she waited with very little patience for Sarah to respond to her question. Alicia kept her eyes fixed on the aged face, as though that visual contact could lessen the blow she knew was coming. Slowly Sarah sat in the upright chair beside the desk and once again attempted to shred her handkerchief into little pieces.

"Alicia," she quavered, "some madman is threatening Clinton's life."

Alicia felt every muscle in her body clench, and she shook her head in disbelief. When Clint had mentioned the crank calls he was receiving, he'd never said one word about them being life threatening. This put an entirely new construction on the situation, and she could hardly reassure Sarah when she needed reassurance herself. Taking a deep breath, she asked, "Who would want to kill him?"

"I don't know," Sarah cried piteously, "and I'm almost out of my mind with worry. I thought the calls had stopped or I would have talked to you about them this past weekend. But they haven't, Alicia. Last evening he . . . he . . ."

"Have you informed Clint?"

Sarah nodded. "I left a message at his hotel and he phoned me back last night."

"What did he say?"

"He told me he'd ask Edna to stay with me until he got home," Sarah said with an indignant gasp. "As though I could be concerned with myself at a time like this!"

Edna was the ranch foreman's wife, and Alicia nodded in silent approval of Clint's actions. Although she'd sometimes accused him of neglecting his mother, she knew the accusation was unfair. His corporation demanded constant attention but he'd always been conscious of Sarah's needs. Sarah had once mentioned to Alicia that Clint wanted to hire a companion for her but that she didn't want some stranger living in her home.

Sarah was nervous when Clint was away but she was too shy to take easily to people she didn't know. With this in mind, Alicia's voice held gentle understanding when she asked, "Have you received any calls today?"

The handkerchief was lifted to a nose already reddened from weeping. "The phone began ringing while Edna and I were having breakfast, and . . . Oh, Alicia, what am I going to do? The beast's voice was muffled to disguise it, and he sounded horrible . . . horrible!"

"Has Clint contacted the police?"

"Clinton refused to take the threats seriously, so I called them."

Alicia's mouth twisted wryly. "I bet he loved that."

"He wasn't too happy with me," Sarah admitted sheepishly. But then her mouth firmed and the line of her jaw angled in a stubborn gesture reminiscent of her son. "I'm not sorry I did it!"

"What did they say?"

Sarah waved the handkerchief wildly in the air and frowned with an unusual degree of ferocity. "Since there's no real evidence of a threat, they said there isn't much they can do at present."

"What?" she exclaimed angrily.

Sarah nodded jerkily and several strands of graying hair escaped from their once tidy bun. Her hands shook as she attempted to restore order to her appearance, only to give up with an impatient grimace. "I'm supposed to use our recorder for all incoming calls in case the man phones again. They said in most cases threats of this nature are a prank. Do you think that's true, Alicia?"

She winced at the pleading note in Sarah's voice and tried to keep her own fear at bay. "I suppose it could be," she replied hesitantly, "but I don't think Clint should take any chances."

"Yet the obstinate man refused to talk to the authorities or take any measures to protect himself. When I tried to reason with him he just laughed and told me not to read any more murder mysteries."

That figures, Alicia decided indignantly as she walked around her desk and seated herself on its edge. Clint was a law unto himself and entirely too sure of his own invincibility. She began to chew at her bottom lip, a frown scoring her forehead as she tried to think. Finally she straightened and said abruptly, "He should hire a bodyguard."

"Can you see Clint allowing a burly man in a tan overcoat to dog his footsteps?"

Alicia grinned at Sarah's description. "You do read too many murder mysteries," she said, but immediately the smile fell from her face. She sighed in frustration. "But you're right. I can't visualize Clint letting anyone tail him."

"Alicia, maybe you can make Clinton see sense."

"I seriously doubt it," she muttered, "but I'm going to give it a darn good try."

"Oh, darling, I knew you'd help."

"I'm not making any promises," she warned quietly. "I have less influence over Clint than you do."

Sarah looked strangely complacent. "I wouldn't say that, dear."

Alicia narrowed her eyes suspiciously. "What's he been telling you?"

"I don't know what in the world you're talking about."

Sarah jumped guiltily when Alicia leaned toward her. "Don't play the innocent with me," she muttered. "You've got a very odd look in your eye, Mrs. Kelly."

"Oh, very well," Sarah responded huffily. "If you must know, before he went back east Clinton told me he'd asked you to marry him."

There was subdued rage in Alicia's low tones as she asked, "Did he also tell you I refused his proposal?"

Sarah's voice was nearly indistinguishable when she admitted, "Yes, but he said he'd wear you down in the end."

Alicia exploded. "He what?"

This time Sarah's reply was spoken in firmer tones. "He said he'd—"

"I heard you the first time," Alicia said through clenched teeth.

Sarah looked indignant. "Then why make me repeat myself?"

"I am not going to marry him, Sarah."

"But you love him, dear."

Suddenly all the aggression drained out of Alicia, and her shoulders slumped. "Am I that obvious?"

"I've known since you were about fifteen, and if I'd had any doubts you still felt the same they would have been dispelled this afternoon."

"I admit I love him," Alicia said in muffled accents, "but you can stop planning the wedding, Sarah. I'm not ready to fetch his pipe and slippers and pander to his every whim."

"He doesn't smoke a pipe," Sarah retorted with pursed lips. "Nasty, smelly old things."

Alicia gave way to laughter and shook her head ruefully. "Darling, you're priceless."

"That isn't what Clint called me when he discovered I'd phoned the police," Sarah exclaimed with affronted ire.

"I don't imagine it was, but I think you did the right thing."

Since her godmother didn't drive, Alicia asked her how she'd gotten to town. "Edna drove me," she replied. Then she hesitated and admitted with a rather sheepish smile, "I told her you'd take me home."

Laughter once again bubbled from Alicia's throat, and she shook her head in mock reproof. "That sure of me, were you?"

Sarah reached over and patted her arm. "Of course, dear."

"Sarah, your hands are like ice," Alicia exclaimed in concern. When the older woman resumed her position in the chair with a tired sigh, Alicia got to her feet and walked across the room. "This has all been a shock to you, but everything is going to be all right. You know how good I am at badgering Clint until I get my own way, so don't worry about a thing. You just sit there and relax while I get a pot of coffee going."

"I could use a cup if it's not too much trouble."

While Alicia fixed the percolator she thought about what she'd said to Sarah. She had a feeling she was being overconfident, since no one knew better than she how stubborn Clint could be once his mind was made up. Only in this instance, she decided resolutely, he wasn't going to be given any choice. Prank caller or not, he couldn't afford to take any chances.

Peeking over her shoulder at Sarah, she was relieved to notice that the older woman seemed much calmer. In fact, she seemed to have almost an air of excitement about her. With a shrug of her shoulders Alicia returned to her task and was soon walking toward Sarah with two brightly colored ceramic mugs in her hands.

Offering Sarah her drink, Alicia once again perched on the edge of the desk and cradled her own mug between her palms. She savored the warmth and began to take tiny sips of the reviving liquid. There was a lot to be said in favor of a good jolt of caffeine, she thought in amusement. If the truth be told, her own hands were as cold as Sarah's had been.

For a while silence reigned, both women lost in thought as they drank their coffee. Then Sarah placed her empty mug on the desk and gave Alicia a small nod of appreciation. "You don't know how much better I feel now that I've talked to you. When I walked in here I was at my wit's end, but now I think I've come up with the perfect solution to our problem.''

Alicia started and glanced at her godmother's beaming features. Sarah had that certain look in her eye and Alicia had a feeling she wasn't going to like what was coming. Her suspicions were justified when Sarah chirped brightly, ''Alicia, you can be Clinton's bodyguard!''

Alicia almost fell off the desk. ''What did you say?''

''I said—''

''I heard you,'' Alicia interrupted.

''That is a most annoying habit of yours,'' Sarah complained primly. ''If you heard the first time, why keep questioning me?''

Alicia ignored the reprimand, her manner distracted as she took a last swallow of coffee and thumped the mug down beside Sarah's. ''I'm a karate instructor, not a bodyguard.''

''You can spend your vacation at the ranch,'' Sarah exclaimed eagerly. ''You know you'd rather be there than all alone at some sandy old beach.''

Alicia gazed at her grimly. ''I like sand.''

''It's unsanitary,'' Sarah remarked. ''Think of the fleas.''

''I like fleas,'' Alicia continued doggedly.

Sarah wasn't put off by Alicia's uncooperative attitude. ''With you there I wouldn't be so frightened.''

At this admission Alicia's expression softened. "Of course I'll stay at the ranch with you, at least until I can convince Clint to hire someone to protect him."

Sarah's relief was palpable. "I know he'll take your advice, dear."

Alicia only wished she could be as certain.

Chapter Seven

Clint strode restlessly across the living room car-
pet, then leaned distractedly against a cherry-paneled
wall. Above his head was a beautifully executed oil
painting of a field of golden poppies against a back-
drop of blue sky and white clouds. Alicia noted that
the scene only seemed to enhance his brooding
countenance.

"Alicia, you and my mother are making mountains out of molehills," he said impatiently. "I don't
need a damned bodyguard."

Alicia smiled with innocent sweetness, but her tone
was sarcastic when she spoke. "And you are the king
of the cliché—I mean mountain."

"Like hell I am," he roared indignantly. "Will you just shut up and listen for a change?"

Her eyes sparkled with humor as she plumped up the rose-colored cushion she was lounging against and made herself more comfortable against the corner of the chintz sofa. "I always listen to you."

"Like hell you do!"

"My, my," she drawled maddeningly, thoroughly pleased with her successful needling of the great man. "Getting repetitious in your old age, aren't you?"

"Like hell I—" He silenced himself abruptly and gave her a look that could have blistered the hide off a rhinoceros. With a muttered oath he again began moving, finally ending up in front of the wide fireplace.

She and Clint had covered nearly this same ground more than an hour ago, and Alicia was getting tired of arguing and trading insults with him. "You are the most obstinate, pigheaded—"

"I agree with Alicia," Sarah interjected hastily, her spine straightening against the cushioned back of her favorite chair. Evidently she was determined to prevent the impending mayhem that was clearly indicated in Clint's expression. "You aren't the only one involved in this situation, Clinton. You should have more concern for my safety, as well as Alicia's."

The movement of his fingers against the intricately carved mantel was suddenly arrested in midtap. "You won't be here."

"Of course I'll be here," Sarah remarked with a brief frown. "This is my home."

Clint didn't bother elaborating, but simply lifted his eyes toward the beamed ceiling in exasperation. After a momentary pause he lowered his gaze to his mother's face and responded to the last part of her earlier statement. "Anyway, what does Alicia have to do with this?"

Alicia stifled a groan as Sarah informed him happily, "If you won't hire someone, she's going to stay here and watch out for your welfare."

Alicia slitted her eyes when his booming laughter rang out. "And just what's so funny about that?" she demanded furiously.

Clint gestured toward her, his glance raking her slight frame as she hunched her body defensively and glared at him. "The idea of you playing bodyguard," he hooted mockingly. "What shall I call you—my guardian angel?"

"Very amusing," she muttered, feeling rebellion seething within her. She swung her head toward Sarah. "Didn't I tell you he'd find the idea hilarious if we said anything to him?"

With a change of mood that left his mother and Alicia staring at him in surprise, he retorted, "I find the idea damned ludicrous."

"But Clinton," Sarah protested hastily, "Alicia's been well trained in the martial arts."

"And taking firsts in organized competitions qualifies her to be a bodyguard?" he questioned silkily, with an oblique glance at Alicia that made her fume. "Not bloody likely!"

"I never said I was qualified," she snapped furiously, "but if you're going to be stupid about this I don't see that I have much choice. Somebody has to take care of you."

With startling swiftness Clint's mood shifted once again, and he gave Alicia a loving look that made her cheeks burn. "I didn't realize I mattered that much to you, my darling."

"I—you—" Alicia stopped spluttering and fixed him with a warning look, her gaze shifting from him to Sarah with unmistakable meaning.

Clint lifted a peremptory hand, his grin showing his white teeth to advantage. But before he could make some audacious remark Sarah exclaimed impatiently, "Of course you matter to her, Clinton. Alicia loves you, although why she should when all you do is tease her is more than I can understand."

His eyes were glinting with suppressed mirth when he turned toward Alicia. "Do you love me, Angel?"

Alicia was tempted to box his ears. "Might I remind you that this is no laughing matter, Clinton?"

"So proper," he murmured mockingly. "Soon I'm going to have to do something to take the starch out of your undies, sweetheart."

"Clinton!" Sarah gasped.

His head swiveled in his mother's direction and he grinned at her unrepentantly. "Just a figure of speech, Mother."

"Then curb your tongue," she ordered affrontedly. "There's no need to be vulgar."

"Yes, ma'am," he intoned with solemn deference. But his mischievously revealing eyes met Alicia's and before she could prevent it a tiny giggle escaped from her mouth. It was followed by another, and soon she and Clint were laughing so hard they could hardly draw breath.

"Well! If you two are going to behave in this nonsensical manner I might as well go to bed."

Neither Clint nor Alicia objected. Both could see the exhaustion that had deepened the lines in Sarah's face, and each in turn gave her a good-night kiss accompanied by a rueful apology. "We're thoughtless monsters," Alicia remarked cheerfully.

Clint nodded his agreement. "We're a couple of toads, Mother."

Sarah stifled a yawn with her hand, while Alicia just stifled herself as her godmother straightened slowly and rose from the cavernous depths of her armchair. "I didn't get much sleep last night and the two of you yammering at each other has given me a headache."

She walked to the foot of the stairs and turned toward them with a stern expression on her face. "I hope you will have reached some kind of compromise by morning. If not, I'm going to refuse to leave my room!"

As soon as Sarah was out of sight, Alicia let go of the grin she'd been hiding behind trembling fingers and gasped incredulously. "A couple of toads?"

Clint returned her smile with interest, and the unholy gleam of amusement she'd spotted earlier deepened in his eyes. "Horny toads, darling."

Alicia's mouth opened, closed and then opened again on a groan. "You are incorrigible!"

"And obstinate, pigheaded..." He cocked his head to the side. "Do you want to add anything else?"

She scowled up at him. "I could go on for hours but I'm not going to waste any more time."

"Mmm," he murmured huskily, moving to sit beside her. "You're right. We are wasting time."

Her breath caught in her throat as he leaned toward her, his arm encircling her shoulders as his mouth zeroed in on her throat. She pushed at his chest, trying to avoid his gently nipping teeth. "Will you get your mind off sex and back to the matter at hand?"

With expert rapidity his fingers tickled their way up her rib cage and settled just below her left breast. As his thumb began to rub the hardening crest through her blue cotton blouse, he whispered, "Anything to please you, Angel."

Clint was pleasing her too damned much, she decided with a shiver of response. Barely preventing her recalcitrant body from arching into his hand, she said sternly, "If you really want to make me happy you'll hire a bodyguard."

He drew back with a resigned sigh, and she knew a momentary regret when his skillfully arousing fingers left her body to brush his tumbled hair away from his forehead. "Alicia, I'm pretty certain I know who's behind these threats and I really don't believe we have anything to worry about. The guy is trying to use scare tactics to pay me back for something he thinks I did, but he hasn't got the guts to follow through. His sort likes to prey on the weak and helpless, and I'm far from being either."

She leaned against his side and began fiddling with the buttons on his white shirt. "Why does he hate you so much, Clint?"

"His wife once worked for me," he admitted with obvious reluctance, "and when she left him he convinced himself we'd been having an affair."

Absently she ran her nails over the crisp dark hair on his upper chest and lifted her head to study his stern expression. "The man's an idiot," she said quietly. "You wouldn't fool around with a married woman."

He caressed her smooth forehead with his mouth. "Thank you for the vote of confidence, honey."

She pulled back to look at him with a frown. "Whatever gave him an idea like that in the first place?"

"About two years ago she came to the office with a black eye and bruises on her face."

Alicia grimaced with distaste. "I think I'm getting the picture."

"Yes," he interjected grimly. "Usually he hit her where no one would see the marks, but according to Susan he was drunker than usual that night and forgot to use caution."

"Her last name wouldn't be Brewster, would it?"

"Yes," he said, his surprise evident. "You know her?"

"Susan was one of my students." Her low voice was full of pity when she continued. "She was always a loner and I suspected there was something terribly wrong in her life. I used to watch her when she worked out, because I had learned to spot the ones who want to learn more than a sport."

"Are there many of them?"

She gave a sigh of resignation. "Too many, Clint. They're not all abused wives, or even necessarily female. Some are victims of violent crimes. In a way, learning to defend themselves gives them back the self-respect they've forfeited through no fault of their own. It also helps to restore their courage and confidence."

Clint tilted her chin back until her face was completely visible, then nodded his approval. "Susan finally drew from that courage," he told her. "If they confide in you, do you counsel them?"

"No, but I put them in touch with someone qualified to help them cope with their difficulties. Susan was too used to keeping her emotions bottled up inside herself to discuss her situation with me. I worried about her a lot and was trying to gain her trust. But she disappeared and I never saw her again. I always wondered what had happened to her."

"She's living in Philadelphia."

Alicia lifted her hand to his face and gently stroked his jaw. "Don't you have a plant in Philly?"

A flush darkened his cheek and he muttered gruffly, "All right, so I gave her a transfer. She was one of the best secretaries I'd ever had and she deserved a promotion. She's now become practically indispensable to Logan Markham, who's president of my board of directors and a good friend of mine. He never stops singing her praises when we get together." Clint chuckled lightly and shook his head. "How such a timid little thing can handle Logan so deftly I'll never understand. He's a bit of a tyrant in the office."

"So are you," she responded dryly.

"Do you think that's why he and I get along so well?"

"I think Logan sounds like you—strong, dependable and a good enough friend to look out for Susan. Am I right, you old softie?"

At her question Clint began to bluster defensively. "Don't go all sentimental and mushy on me, Alicia. I told you, I didn't want the corporation to lose a damn good secretary!"

"Don't get a hitch in your getalong just because I admire what you did for Susan," she reprimanded him. "She was too shy and introverted to break free on her own."

"With good reason," he said cryptically.

"It makes me sick to think of a man using brute strength on someone so defenseless."

Clint nodded, his gaze hardening as he stared across the room. Alicia could tell he wasn't really seeing the gold-framed antique mirror above the mantel or the soothing tint of the pale apricot walls. "She was so terrified of him it took me quite a while to get the whole story out of her."

"What did you do then?"

"I took her to a divorce lawyer, and we got a police injunction to prevent her husband from going anywhere near her. Then we collected some bare essentials from her home and I drove her to a shelter for battered women."

She snuggled closer to him, her voice choked with emotion when she said, "Sometimes you're a pretty special guy, Mr. Kelly. Are you aware of that?"

Clint gave a disgusted snort, but he tightened his arm around her. "Why, because I don't like the idea of any woman being victimized in that way?"

"No," she whispered softly, "because you had the courage to do something about it."

His eyes followed the movement of her mouth. "Are you going to reward me?"

"Don't push your luck," she retorted with a grin. "Right now I'm feeling very benevolent toward you but it might not last long."

He gave an exaggerated sigh and shook his head ruefully. "It never does."

"Anyway, so Susan's husband blames you for his wife leaving him. Why should he connect you with the divorce?"

"Because a neighbor described me to him when I took Susan home to help her pack," he said tonelessly. "Brewster and I had been introduced at the company Christmas party the previous year, so he knew right away who she was talking about. But even if that interfering old busybody had kept her mouth shut I would have been a marked man. According to Susan he was insanely jealous and was always accusing her of having affairs with other men. After he met me he became more convinced than ever but he wouldn't let her quit her job. On the contrary," he muttered in disgust. "He was too fond of the income she brought in."

Alicia didn't look at all surprised. Aware of the devastating charm and good looks Clint possessed in abundance, she would have been amazed if Susan's husband hadn't been jealous. "You shouldn't sound so disparaging," she said with mock indignation. "You're a very sexy guy."

He seemed startled by the admission and his voice sounded gruff when he asked, "Do you think I'm sexy?"

She slanted him a provocative glance from under her lashes. "I plead the Fifth."

Clint nipped at the lobe of her ear. "Maybe you need a little convincing."

He proceeded to convince her with a thoroughness that left Alicia pliant and moaning in his arms. When the kiss ended she stared up at him with bemusement. Suddenly remembering the subject of their conversation, she frowned. With a sigh she whispered, "Poor Susan. I wonder if she ever felt this way with her husband?"

Clint shook his head, his eyes mirroring her disquiet. "I doubt it," he replied. "Susan told me that when she first started dating Neil he treated her like a fairy princess, but soon his aggressive tendencies began to show. The night she tried to break up with him he raped her, and when she ended up pregnant her parents kicked up quite a fuss."

"I didn't know she had a child."

"She didn't," Clint remarked with a terrible anger in his eyes. "The first time he beat her she miscarried. I told you he always hit her where it didn't show."

Horrified by this revelation, Alicia burst out, "Oh, God! Why didn't she leave him then?"

"He used her younger sister as the ace up his sleeve and Susan was too terrified of him not to believe he'd do what he threatened."

In a voice that shook, Alicia whispered, "He threatened to rape the girl, too, didn't he?"

"A thirteen-year-old kid," Clint said disgustedly. "Some man, Mr. Neil Brewster."

Alicia swallowed, feeling sick. "The child, he hasn't...?"

"Her mother and father agreed to let Susan take her with her to Philadelphia." He shook his head, his low tone holding derision as he muttered, "If the understanding and support toward their oldest daughter was any indication, they weren't much use as parents anyway. Carlie is much better off being raised by her sister."

Alicia closed her eyes in relief. "Susan was right to be afraid for Carlie. I think any man who beats a woman is basically uncertain of his masculinity, and Neil sounds like a particularly brutal individual. Clint, if he's as unbalanced as I suspect, you've got to agree to take precautions to ensure your safety."

"Now, Angel..."

"Don't you now Angel me, Clinton Kelly." She tugged viciously at the black, crinkly hair protruding from the collar of his shirt. "If you think I'm going to stand by while some madman blows you away, you've got another think coming."

"Ouch, that hurt, you little devil!" Clint held her head still by squeezing her chin between his thumb and forefinger. "How did you know he threatened to shoot me?"

Alicia glared up at him and refused to answer. "My mother," he muttered grimly. "I wish she hadn't dragged you into this, babe. I was going to send her to stay with her friend in San Francisco until—"

"Then you are taking this threat seriously," Alicia retorted triumphantly.

Clint's lips twisted in rueful acknowledgment. "Let's just say I wasn't going to take any chances with my mother's safety. I'm not that pigheaded."

"Oh, yes you are," she contradicted heatedly. "If you weren't you'd be thinking of your own safety. Instead you're just going to—"

"Hire a bodyguard," he interrupted.

"—stay here like a sitting duck. What did you say?"

He gave her a resigned glance, but there was a trace of defensiveness in his voice as he muttered, "I said

I'm going to hire a bodyguard. Otherwise I'll have you and my mother breathing fire down my neck."

Alicia nodded and grinned up at him. "Every minute of every day," she agreed with irritating complacence.

"Don't rub my nose in it."

She stretched her body and landed a kiss on the item in question, remarking teasingly, "It's big enough."

One corner of his mouth lifted as he gave her bottom a pinch. "I'm a big man."

Alicia glared indignantly at him and rubbed her backside. "That hurt!"

"You pulled the hair on my chest."

"That's different," she contradicted crossly.

"Do you want me to kiss it and make it better?" he asked softly.

Alicia moistened her lips with the tip of her tongue and gave his chest a lingering glance. "Do you want me to?"

Clint began to flick open the buttons on his shirt. Excitement flared in her eyes when he pulled the fabric free of his jeans. "Does this answer your question?"

Again Alicia's tongue darted out to bathe her lower lip. Her chest was rising and falling with the force of her escalating emotions. Apparently taking in the signs of her arousal, Clint groaned his approval as he stared at her mouth. "Do that to me, Angel."

With the sluggishness of preoccupation she lifted her head, and her trembling increased at the expression in his eyes. "Do what?" she asked timorously.

"Touch me with your tongue," he urged, his voice a low growl of anticipation.

Obediently she bent forward and began to lave his small, hard nipple with eager curiosity. Alicia was enjoying his taste and texture and the delicious musky fragrance rising from his body. She was also enjoying the power she had over him as he moaned in her arms.

"Like this?" she murmured provocatively.

"Alicia," he gulped in strangulated accents, "I don't think this was such a good idea."

She spread both her hands over the thick pelt covering his chest, and mewed a protest. "I think it was a wonderful idea. I love touching you, Clint. Why don't you touch me back?"

"But I want to do more than touch you," he uttered harshly, "and now is not the time."

As though he couldn't stop himself, he enclosed her flushed cheeks between his palms. His head blotted out the lights recessed into the beamed ceiling as he sought her mouth with undeniable hunger. His lips slanted over hers, brushing back and forth with a slow cadence that drove her over the edge.

"Kiss me," she gasped. "Kiss me hard, Clint."

Alicia was shuddering like a willow frond in a windstorm as she shifted up on her knees to get closer to him. Now she was instigating the depth of the kiss, showing him what she'd learned from him such a short time ago. Her arms wrapped themselves around his neck like a vise and she slipped her tongue into his mouth with a muffled sound of pleasure. Their tongues began dueling with provocative abandon and Clint's hands slipped down to cup her breasts.

Then his mouth was on her throat, shifting hurriedly to the V of her blouse like a thirsty man seeking water. "We'd better not have too long an engagement," he muttered with wry emphasis. "Much more of this kind of frustration and I'll be a blithering idiot. It's a good thing you're not going to be around for a while."

Alicia felt as if she'd suddenly been doused with a bucket of ice water. "What do you mean I'm not going to be around?"

Clint felt her body stiffen and leaned his head back against the sofa to stare up at her in surprise. "I just meant that since I've agreed to hire a bodyguard you can leave on your vacation with an easy mind."

Alicia pulled away from him, her eyes never straying from his face as she resumed sitting by his side. "Oh, I can, can I?"

Puzzled by the grim note in her voice, he nodded. "Do you think you could drop my mother off in San Francisco before you head for Santa Cruz?"

"You just expect me to waltz away on my vacation," she intoned with what she felt was admirable calmness, "knowing I'm leaving you alone here to face a crazy man?"

"I won't be alone," he responded with escalating impatience. "I'll have your damned bodyguard here and the police will be patrolling the ranch at regular intervals."

"Sarah said they weren't being very cooperative."

"They were when I showed them the notes I've been receiving at the office this past month."

Alicia's eyes widened and her face paled. "He's written to you?"

He gave a short bark of laughter and shook his head. "Nothing so mundane. It must have taken him hours to cut out the letters from magazines and newspapers. He glued them to common pieces of typing paper so the letter couldn't be traced, and since there were no fingerprints he probably wore gloves of some sort. He must read the same kind of books my mother enjoys."

Alicia gave an indignant hiss through her clenched teeth. "So you were taking this man's threat seriously all along. Why did you lie to Sarah and me?"

"I didn't want either of you involved, but the bastard ruined my plans when he started calling here."

"He certainly did."

Clint registered her mutinous expression and his own features became wary. "I don't like that look in your eyes, Angel."

Her mouth took on a smug curve and she crossed her arms over her chest in a gesture of defiance. "Don't you mean guardian angel, Clint?"

"What's that supposed to mean?"

"Can't you guess?" she responded with a complacent smile. In triumphant tones she informed him, "It means I'm not setting one foot off this ranch until that creep is put away."

"We'll see," Clint said with deceptive quiescence.

Alicia gave him an uncertain smile, and swallowed nervously when he failed to respond.

Chapter Eight

Alicia burst into Clint's study, the expression on her face boding ill for the man lounging indolently in a deep, cushioned plaid chair situated close to the French doors that led onto the veranda. "What does Sarah mean," she began without preamble, "you've invited Kevin and Jane for dinner?"

Clint glanced up from the book he was reading, one dark eyebrow lifting in mild query. His hair was still damp from the shower he'd taken and the pale lemon pullover sweater he was wearing emphasized his dark tan. Alicia thought he appeared devastatingly attractive, which didn't aid her sense of outrage when he teased, "Is that such an unusual occurrence?"

"Don't sound so innocent." Since she was having trouble preventing herself from rushing across the room to run her fingers over the soft cashmere material covering his strong, muscular chest, her voice sounded more strident than she'd intended when she accused, "You deliberately kept me riding all afternoon so I wouldn't find out until the last minute."

"You love taking the horses for a run."

"Not until my thighs are rubbed raw and my bottom bruised," she retorted with a disdainful sniff. "I've been in the tub over an hour and I'm still sore."

"Poor baby," he soothed with an infuriating lack of sympathy. "I've got some ointment that'll fix you up as good as new."

Alicia gestured to the blue chiffon dress she wore and scowled at him. "I'm already dressed for dinner, and don't change the subject."

"What subject is that, Angel Face?"

Alicia took his expression of endearment as an insult, since she knew her features were far from angelic at the moment. Stomping over to his chair, she hovered over him threateningly and spoke one name. "Kevin."

"I'm only returning his hospitality," he explained with a facile charm that grated quite dreadfully on her nerves. "If you remember, I had dinner with him and Jane before my trip back east."

Alicia remembered the outcome of that dinner invitation very well, and she flushed as she encountered his mocking stare. Just thinking about his jealous reaction to her dating Charlie Keel made her go hot all over. Angling her jaw mutinously, she insisted, "You've got something up your sleeve, Clinton."

"Now who's dealing in clichés?" he grinned. "What nefarious plot do you think I'm hatching?"

"You're going to sic Kevin on me!"

He gave a bellow of laughter that made her want to smack him a good one. Before she could give in to the urge the doorbell rang, and she gave him a fulminating glare before going to answer it. The instant she saw Jane's face her suspicions regarding Clint's motives were quite adequately confirmed.

To say her sister-in-law was nervous was an understatement. She kept snapping the catch on her purse with restless fingers and her lips barely twitched in uneasy acknowledgment of Alicia's greeting. As for her brother, he looked as though he'd swallowed one of Clint's horny toads.

Alicia stood back so they could enter. As she took Jane's coat and began to hang it in the hall closet, she glanced over her shoulder at Kevin. "Clint's in his study if you'd like to join him."

"You come along, too," Kevin demanded in a tightly controlled voice. "There's something important we need to talk about, and if that guilty expression on your face is any indication, you're well aware of the reason I'm here tonight."

"I thought you came for dinner."

"Don't be insolent," Kevin retorted heatedly. "You're too old for such childish behavior."

"But I'm not too old to be ordered around?" she inquired with ominous quietness.

The sound of a throat being cleared drew their attention, and both Alicia and her brother stared uncomprehendingly at Jane. "I hate to spoil your impending shouting match, but will you two take time out to remember you love each other?"

Neither of the protagonists could resist the truth behind the gentle reproof, but resentment still simmered between them as they watched each other with wary restraint. Several moments passed, each more fraught with tension than the last. Finally Kevin, giving an exasperated sigh, sought to explain his aggressive behavior to his wife.

"It's because I love her that I'm worried," he admitted impatiently. "Why is every suggestion I make met with an argument?"

"Because you don't suggest," Alicia interjected with hostility. "You order, Kevin."

He rubbed the back of his neck and smiled ruefully. "Then may I request your presence in Clint's study for a moment, Alicia?"

She shot a panicky look at Jane, who immediately turned to her husband with a strained smile.

"All that can wait until after dinner. Alicia and I are going to go help Sarah in the kitchen."

Before Kevin could protest, Alicia took advantage of the reprieve Jane had given her and began dragging her sister-in-law down the hall. Once they had rounded the corner and were out of Kevin's sight, Alicia sagged against the wall and closed her eyes. "I'm going to kill Clint!"

Jane's concern was clearly evident when she remarked, "According to what he told Kevin, someone's threatening to do just that."

When Alicia's lashes lifted they were spiked with revealing moisture. "Oh, Jane," she whispered on a sob. "I'm so terrified for him."

Jane's eyes glowed with scarcely concealed satisfaction. "I wondered how long it was going to take you to admit it."

It wasn't difficult for Alicia to catch the drift of Jane's thoughts, but she was too keyed up at the moment to give in gracefully. With a petulant slant to her mouth she exclaimed, "Your imagination is running overtime, Mrs. Mason."

"Is it?" Jane asked with an understanding smile and a shake of her head. "Somehow I don't think so, little sister."

Alicia stiffened her spine and tried to straighten to five-foot-one. With a resentful sniff she said, "I think Kevin's beginning to rub off on you, Janey."

Jane arched a quizzical eyebrow, her eyes intense as she gazed at Alicia. "You mean you aren't in love with Clint?"

Unable to lie, Alicia used evasion as the best method of defense. "The man is as irritating as poison oak."

Jane placed her hands on her slender hips. "Then he must have a matching itch, because you've been driving him crazy for years. Even your brother knows how Clint feels about you."

Alicia's mouth formed a startled O. "How can he?" she questioned in disbelief. "I didn't know myself until a couple of weeks ago."

At this admission Jane gave her a teasing look. "I thought I was imagining things."

"You...I..." Alicia took a deep breath and counted to ten before taking another tack. Deliberately assuming a defensive pose, arms crossed and eyes narrowed, she asked, "Just how did Kevin find out about Clint and me?"

Jane gave a nervous giggle and slammed her hand over her mouth. "Oops!"

Alicia glanced at her sister-in-law in horror. "Jane, you didn't...?"

"Of course not," Jane retorted, managing to appear hurt and indignant at the same time. "Since when have I ever betrayed your confidence—especially when you've never confided your feelings to me?"

Alicia cringed inwardly, ashamed of her past reticence with a woman who had become a combination of mother and big sister to her over the years. With a contrite expression, she whispered, "I didn't want to admit the truth, even to myself. I never meant to hide anything from you, Janey."

"Then you are in love with Clint."

It was a statement not a question, and Alicia responded accordingly. "Yes."

The single word held more effect than any lengthier explanation could have, and Jane placed a consoling hand on Alicia's arm. "Why haven't you wanted to admit how you feel?"

"Because if I let him, Clint will take over my entire life, Jane."

"Don't worry, darling," she encouraged. "I felt many of the same reservations when I met Kevin, but I've managed to handle him. Believe me, you won't be jumping from the frying pan into the fire when you marry Clint."

Another cliché, Alicia thought with a touch of hysteria. Controlling herself with an effort, she gave a defiant toss of her head. "I'm not marrying him, Jane."

"You mean he hasn't asked you?" she asked in surprise. "But he told us he intended to—"

Alicia gasped and jerked her hand back. "Just when did this little family conclave take place?"

The grim inflection in her voice caused Jane to shift nervously and avoid Alicia's eyes. "I never said..." she began weakly.

"You've never been able to lie your way out of a paper bag," Alicia interrupted, hardening her heart against the vivid appeal in Jane's widening gaze. "I expect an answer, Janey."

With a frustrated sigh the other woman complied. "Clint told Kevin he was going to ask you to marry him the last time we were together."

"Ahh, the infamous dinner party," Alicia remarked bitterly. "I take it my brother agreed?"

Jane nodded, a guilty flush dotting her cheeks. "It wasn't the way it seems, Alicia. Naturally Clint wanted Kevin's approval before he proposed to you."

"Why naturally?" Alicia asked, her anger barely held in check. "For heaven's sake, we're not living in the Dark Ages. I should have been the first person to be consulted, not my brother. But as usual those two sat down and decided my future without a word to me. Well, I turned Clint down, which is something he and my autocratic brother had better accept."

Jane clutched at her throat and gave her a look of utter disbelief. "You didn't!"

"I most certainly did."

Admitting the truth to Jane affirmed Alicia's decision, and she felt sudden regret claw at her. Why couldn't Clint be easygoing and reasonable like other men? she wondered painfully. If only he weren't so arrogantly set in his ways there might be a chance for them to have a future together. But knowing Clint as well as she did, she knew he'd never change.

Would you want him to, Alicia? a little voice questioned from the back of her mind. Don't you already love him the way he is, and not as you want him to be?

Yes, she replied in silent rebellion, but that doesn't mean I could stand living with him!

As though able to read her mind, Jane insisted, "But you love him and he loves you." She shook her head in bewildered dismay. "You two are perfect for each other, darling."

Alicia clenched her hands into fists at her sides. "We are completely unsuited, whatever you may think, Jane. We're both stubborn with tempers to match, and we'd be doing more fighting than loving if we married."

Jane gave her a shrewd look. "From what I've learned of Clint over the years, I rather doubt that."

"Oh, I'll admit that he wants me," she retorted with exasperated honesty.

Jane frowned in perplexity. "Of course he does."

Alicia fought to subdue her embarrassment and began to chew the "Bewitching Berry" lipstick from her mouth. "There's more to a relationship than sex, Janey. Clint wants me physically, but he doesn't need me emotionally."

Jane began to look somewhat confused. "Men aren't as open about their emotions as women, Alicia. I'm certain Clint needs you as much as you need him."

"Hah!" Alicia burst out in goaded accents. "All he wants is to get me into bed with him."

"I understand that part of it," Jane responded with goaded emphasis, "but what I don't understand is your reaction. Sharing a bed is the normal procedure when a man and a woman want each other."

"Not when that woman is his mother's godchild. If it weren't for Sarah and his friendship with Kevin, Clint would just try to make me his mistress and go on with his satisfying bachelor existence."

"I think you're wrong," Jane insisted stubbornly.

Much to Alicia's relief, Sarah chose that moment to bustle out of the kitchen and greet Jane with a hug. "It's good to see you again," she said happily. "Did you just arrive?"

"A few minutes ago," Jane acknowledged, returning the older woman's affectionate embrace with unfeigned enthusiasm. "Alicia and I were on our way to help you with dinner, but I'm afraid we got sidetracked."

She shot Alicia a glance that clearly implied that their conversation was far from over, before turning to grin at Sarah. "What can we do to help?"

"I'm ready to serve," Sarah replied. "If you two would just set the table?"

For Alicia, the meal was a disaster from start to finish. Sarah had prepared leg of lamb, mashed potatoes and gravy, broccoli in a delectable cheese sauce and flaky homemade scones dripping with butter. But with Clint giving her smug looks and her own thoughts in a turmoil, every bite she put into her mouth was tasteless.

Clint she could have dealt with, but it was her brother who was the one most responsible for her lack of appetite. Kevin constantly glowered at her across the snowy white tablecloth, and the steady contemplation by his blue eyes made her fervently wish to be anywhere but where she was—China, Siam, outer space, she wasn't particular. Chewing became a monumental undertaking and swallowing a near impossibility.

Luckily everyone else's digestion was aided by Jane. Well used to the volatile temperaments of her husband and sister-in-law, she had perfected the art of peacemaker over the years. She chattered brightly, covering the strained silences that developed between Alicia and Kevin, as well as Alicia and Clint.

Admiring her sister-in-law's conversational fluency, Alicia fervently hoped Jane wouldn't run out of words before she could make her escape to the kitchen. She should have known better. Kevin waited only until they were nearly finished with dessert to irritably push his plate aside and fix Alicia with a brooding stare.

His unblinking inspection of her was nerve-racking and she betrayed her uneasiness as she wondered what kind of thoughts were running through his mind. Squirming uncomfortably on the tapestry-covered dining-room chair, her fingers trembled as she concentrated on pushing a fragrant slice of blueberry pie around on her plate with a fork.

"So, Alicia," Kevin began quietly enough. "Clint tells me you've decided to vacation here at the ranch."

"Yes," she muttered briefly, glancing over his left shoulder to stare at the antique serving cart that was Sarah's pride and joy.

"Umm, Clint said something about you insisting on staying here to guard him. Would you like to explain?"

The goading irony in her brother's voice caused an angry flush to spread across her cheeks, and she noticed with regret the sudden nervousness in both Sarah and Jane. She hated to spoil the dinner party, but she wasn't about to allow Kevin to browbeat her into submission. Meeting his eyes, she replied to his question with mounting antagonism. "No. I don't wish to explain anything to you, Kevin."

Kevin's handsome features hardened; his voice was barely above a whisper as a he stated incredulously, "You must be out of your mind."

Alicia quickly shoved a bite of pie into her mouth to avoid loudly defending herself, and gave him a cloyingly sweet smile instead. Kevin clasped his fingers together and leaned forward, which was not a sign that boded well for peace of mind. Usually the mannerism denoted suppressed rage, which proved to be the case when he uttered harshly, "Clint and I have talked it over, and we feel Sarah would benefit from your company while all of these threats are being bandied about. The two of you can come and stay with Jane and me for a few weeks."

"If I were going anywhere it would be back to my own apartment," Alicia insisted coolly. "But since I'm not, Sarah might enjoy using it in my absence."

Sarah glanced from Alicia to Kevin, her low tones holding no hesitation as she remarked, "It's sweet of you and Jane to be concerned about me, Kevin, but Alicia's right. I'm not going to leave my son and I won't be frightened if Alicia's staying here. Anyway, Clinton is going to hire a professional bodyguard so I'm certain we'll all be perfectly safe."

Alicia wanted to give her godmother a rousing cheer but her mouth was still full of pie. Washing the overly masticated lump down her throat with a sip of coffee, she nearly gagged when Kevin countered, "But I refuse to allow Alicia to stay here, Sarah."

A crumb that seemed the size of a boulder lodged in Alicia's throat, and it was a while before she had enough breath to protest her brother's high-handedness. Although the resultant coughing fit made her extremely uncomfortable, at least the delay gave her time to collect her thoughts. As she wiped her mouth with a gold linen napkin, her eyes held steely determination. "You forget I'm past the age of needing your consent, Kevin," she said forcefully. "I told Clint I wouldn't leave this ranch until the madman who's threatening him is apprehended and that's exactly the way it's going to be."

Alicia shot Clint a hard glare before returning her attention to her brother. "Clint never should have discussed this with you, but I guess he figured that two dominant males were better than one in forcing me to comply with his wishes."

"No one is going to force you to do anything," Jane promised with an angry look at her husband.

"For God's sake," Clint groaned. "I refuse to allow my mother and Alicia to be placed in danger."

Sarah's head jerked up and her lips tightened before she rejoined the argument. "Might I remind you that this is my home, Clinton. If I don't choose to leave there's nothing you can do about it."

Kevin clenched his jaw and muttered, "Be reasonable, Sarah."

"You mind your own business," Jane retorted.

"Clint and I aren't trying to play the heavies," Kevin exploded. "We're just attempting to take necessary safety precautions where Sarah and Alicia are concerned."

Alicia gave her brother a scathing glance. "You and Clint can stuff your safety precautions."

"Kevin's right, Alicia," Clint remarked in a calm manner meant to restore a little sanity to the conversation. "You and my mother will be better off away from here."

"You told me you weren't worried about these threats," she protested heatedly. "If that's the case, then it shouldn't concern you if I choose to stay here."

Alicia didn't like the look of Clint's smile, which had the quality of a wolf closing in for the kill. "But this is my home," he murmured succinctly, "and I don't want you here."

Sarah gave an indignant gasp. "Then she'll stay as my guest, Clinton!"

After giving her godmother a nod of approval, Alicia returned Clint's smile with interest and resorted to a bribe. "Do you want me to marry you, Clint?"

His eyes narrowed and her skin prickled with nervousness at the enormity of the decision she'd just made. Everyone else at the table seemed frozen in place, collectively holding their breath as Clint remarked with forbidding emphasis, "You'd better know what you're doing, Angel Face. I'm too old for game playing."

Alicia tossed her red-gold curls and held his eyes with her own. "I know exactly what I'm doing."

With a derisive smirk Clint lifted his water glass and proposed a toast. "To my guardian angel," he murmured, "and my future wife."

"Oh, darlings," Sarah cried emotionally, all discord forgotten. "This is the happiest day of my life."

Kevin seemed dazed, Jane bewildered, while the two principal characters in the scenario glared across the table at each other with daggers drawn. Clint's eyes promised retribution at some later date while Alicia's sparkled with unmistakable triumph.

Kevin drank half of his water in three gulps and returned his glass to the table with controlled precision. Then he lifted his head and told Alicia, "Being engaged to Clint hardly reduces the threat to your safety. If anything, it increases your vulnerability. If Clint's right about this joker's identity, we know he wouldn't hesitate to harm a woman. What better way for him to pay Clint back for imagined wrongs than by hurting you?"

"Don't you think I realize that?" Alicia remarked with more patience than she thought she possessed. "I'm not a fool, Kevin."

"Yes, you are," Clint responded angrily. "A brave little fool who doesn't know when to retreat gracefully. You're going home with Kevin tonight and I don't want to hear another word of protest from you."

"That must have been the shortest engagement in history," she interjected mockingly.

"Is that a threat?"

Alicia nodded, her expression composed as she gazed at him. "I'm starting as I mean to go on, Clint. I intend to have an equal say in my marriage and if you don't respect my wishes now you never will. I'm a grown woman with the right to make my own decisions and it's time both you and my brother accepted that fact."

With grave dignity Alicia got to her feet and threw her crumpled napkin down on the table. "Now if you don't mind, I've had enough discussion for one evening. I intend to clean the kitchen, shower and go to bed. You gentlemen can stay here and argue to your heart's content as long as you realize my mind is made up. I'm staying and nothing either of you says is going to make any difference."

Jane jumped up with a delighted grin, completely ignoring the impotent frustration marring her husband's handsome features. Sarah, too, ignored her son's scowling countenance and said firmly, "If they want to argue they can do so in Clinton's study." She collected dishes and silverware and turned to place them on the empty serving tray. "If you'll follow me, ladies?"

Clint and Kevin just sat and stared as Jane, Alicia and Sarah, their backs ramrod straight and their heads lifted proudly, exited the dining room in stately precision. Just before she disappeared around the kitchen door Alicia glanced over her shoulder, noting with satisfaction the identical expressions of stunned incredulity on the faces of the men.

Chapter Nine

Alicia secured the last plate in the dishwasher and wiped down the stove and the gold-veined ceramic-tile counters with extra zeal. Rinsing out the cleaning cloth in the sink, she inspected her pristine surroundings without satisfaction. She prowled restlessly across the floor, skirting the butcher-block table in the center of the room, the tap of her heeled sandals against the shiny surface another irritant to nerves already stretched to the breaking point. Her eyes darted from one side of the kitchen to the other, looking for something more to occupy her hands.

With a moue of impatience, Alicia inwardly berated herself for drinking so much coffee. That was why she was feeling so unsettled, she thought staunchly. It had nothing to do with letting everyone, including Clint, think she intended to marry him. Nor did it have anything to do with the ominous flash she'd seen in his dark eyes when she'd passed him in the hall a few hours ago. No, her tension didn't have a thing to do with that unspoken promise of retribution she'd sensed emanating from him.

With a muttered imprecation she began to dry her hands on the terry-cloth towel hanging from a circular ring beside the refrigerator. As she wiped the moisture from her fingers she reflected on her lack of appetite. During dinner she had done little more than push the food around on her plate—unusual behavior for her. Considering the emotional upheaval going on inside her, if her past record was anything to go by she should be pigging out about now.

Yet in actual fact the thought of food was repulsive since it only reminded her of how foolishly she'd behaved at dinner this evening. How could she have been so incredibly stupid? she wondered sickly. Now she was committed to an engagement that had been no more than a crazy impulse. Not for the first time she asked herself when she was going to learn to keep her temper from controlling her tongue. Probably never, if she spent the rest of her life within shouting distance of Clint, she decided glumly.

If she built up her savings a little, maybe she could eventually open a training studio in another city.

Preferably somewhere in Alaska, or better yet New Zealand, she thought with a cynical smirk. That should be far enough away from Clinton Kelly to keep her sanity intact. Alicia released her grip on the mangled towel and asked herself who she thought she was kidding. She could run as far and as fast as she wanted but there was no way she could ever escape her love for that irritating autocrat.

Without much interest she glanced at the clock on the wall, her eyes widening in surprise. It was nearly midnight. Sarah had long since departed for bed, yet Alicia felt as though her eyelids had been permanently glued into an open position. Her body ached with tiredness. Her stomach was jumping and her head throbbed in time with her heartbeat. Under the circumstances, she thought with a resigned grimace, she doubted if she'd get much sleeping done tonight.

Then she remembered the books she'd brought with her and let out a sigh of relief. One of them had been written by her favorite author, a woman who had yet to disappoint her with either plot or characterization. With any luck she would be able to submerge herself in fantasy and escape her tortured thoughts. But first, she decided, she would take a nice, relaxing shower and get ready for bed. Then she could read until she became drowsy.

With a tingle of anticipation she turned out the lights and quickly climbed the stairs. The smooth oak bannister rail felt cool beneath her hand and when she entered her bedroom she was comforted by its familiarity. After collecting her robe and a thigh-length nightshirt with a slightly tipsy-looking Snoopy emblazoned on the front, she headed down the hall toward the bathroom.

Since the walls were thick and Sarah's room was along the opposite end of the corridor from her own, she wasn't afraid of waking the older woman. But even so she moderated her husky voice as she sang a popular tune while she bathed and washed her hair. She was soothed by the routine activity and her tense muscles began to relax as the deliciously warm water streamed over her body.

By the time she had turned off the taps and dried herself with a large fluffy towel, she felt like a human being again. Well, almost, she amended with a pert grin as she caught sight of her wavering reflection in the steamy mirror. Rubbing the glass with a corner of her damp towel, she frowned at the tangled curls framing her face.

Even with the aid of cream rinse, Alicia usually found getting all of the snarls out of her thick hair a painful process. And although she wasn't in the mood to deal with the tangles right now, she knew better than to go to bed with her hair in this riotous state of disarray. She didn't want to start her morning looking as if she'd been dragged through a hedge.

After she slipped the nightshirt over her head, it only took her five minutes with Sarah's hair dryer and a brush to restore order to her tousled locks. Shaking her head ruefully, she wondered if it was her imagination that made Snoopy's smile seem more like a lustful leer. Immediately reminded of Clint, she giggled as she retraced her steps down the hallway, her feet bare and her robe thrown carelessly over her arm.

Alicia entered her darkened room and reached for the light switch, uttering a stifled cry when someone turned on one of the shaded lamps along the far wall. With a strangled gasp she whirled around so suddenly the door slammed behind her. The unexpected sound caused her to jump, and she was already incensed by her own cowardly behavior when Clint lifted himself from a lounging position on her bed.

"What are you doing here?" she demanded irritably.

His dark hair made a disturbing contrast against the white pillowcases and he was clad in only a pair of rust-colored pajama bottoms. His bare, hair-roughened chest was even more disruptive to her equilibrium than the hair on her pillow. It isn't fair for any one man to have that much physical charisma, she thought resentfully. It just isn't fair!

With an annoyingly amused quirk to his lips he retrieved something from her nightstand and held it up for her inspection. "I told you earlier I had some ointment that would take the pain out of your chafed skin."

So much had happened this evening, it seemed years rather than hours since they'd been out riding together. If it hadn't been for the stinging reminder along the inside of her reddened thighs, she would have wondered what he was talking about. "That's all right," she murmured with forced politeness. "It doesn't hurt anymore."

"Little liar," he accused softly.

Alicia stared at him warily, definitely disturbed by the way he was cyeing her choice of evening attire. She seriously doubted that it was Snoopy's idiotic grin he was fascinated with, and with a frown of disapproval she lifted her robe against her chest. His deep, sexy chuckle at the defensive maneuver didn't do much to help her reassert her shattered composure. With as casual a manner as she could manage without the support of her knees, she stepped closer to him and reached for the tube of ointment resting in his outstretched palm.

The movement was an enormous tactical error. Before she could evade him, he reached around her waist with one burly arm, slipped his other beneath her knees and carried her toward a rose-colored chaise lounge located near the window. Turning on the reading light next to the chaise, he calmly knelt beside her and uncapped the tube of cream.

Still shocked by the suddenness of his actions, Alicia stuttered, "I can d-do it, C-Clint."

His eyes were hooded as he squeezed a generous amount of the medication into his palm. "And deny me the pleasure?"

She scrambled for leverage among the throw pillows against her back, but she might as well not have bothered. With a stern look Clint just pushed her down again and began spreading the ointment against her skin with his other hand. Heat flooded her stomach as she felt his gentle touch against her irritated flesh, his palm rubbing the soothing lotion carefully over the inside of her parted thighs.

Alicia was definitely not soothed. On the contrary, her agitation was increasing to gigantic proportions. Her breathing was growing heavy and slow, and yet her pulse was pounding through her body with the rhythm of a bongo drum. She had the most absurd impulse to guide his magical fingers higher, until his touch cooled the burning sensation building inside her.

It was when she saw the expression on his face as he recapped the tube that she began to bristle with resentment. The smug, self-satisfied curve of his mouth made her realize he was well aware of her response to his ministrations. His concern had been a calculated maneuver to punish her for her recalcitrant attitude this evening, and he'd succeeded beyond his wildest dreams. With a cry of sheer rage she lunged away from him, throwing him off balance with the force of her withdrawal.

But she had miscalculated his agility. She hadn't gone three feet when Clint's steely fingers gripped her wrist and jerked her against his warm body. Intimidated by that devastating expanse of copper-toned flesh so close to her nose, she let out another furious cry of protest. The sound was stifled by his hotly seeking mouth, and when his tongue coaxed her lips to open more widely for his sensual exploration she went limp in his arms.

Both the robe she'd forgotten she was clutching and the tube of ointment dropped to the pale green-carpeted floor, but she didn't notice. With her hands dangling uselessly at her sides, her total concentration seemed to be centered on her throbbing lips. She felt dizzy and disoriented, incapable of denying herself the pleasure of his kiss. When his tensile fingers began to burrow beneath the slightly damp hair at the nape of her neck, she moaned in undeniable arousal.

As though that betraying sound satisfied him, Clint drew his head back and looked at her. His breathing was as ragged as her own, his eyes slumberous as they studied the moist bloom on her swollen lips. "Don't you think you'd be more comfortable in bed?"

The huskily voiced question nearly paralyzed her vocal cords. Clearing her throat so she wouldn't betray her nervousness with an ignominious squeak, Alicia plastered a smile on her face and gave it her best shot. "I have a headache."

Alicia slammed her eyes shut. I didn't say that, she thought despairingly. Tell me I didn't say that! When no answer was forthcoming from the humiliated depths of her psyche, she lifted the veil of her lashes to confront her moment of truth. As she had suspected, Clint was having trouble keeping a straight face.

"All right," she snapped. "You've had your petty revenge, so you can just take yourself and your inflated male ego back to your own room, Mr. Kelly."

"Now why should my ego need inflating, my darling? Didn't you make me the happiest man alive tonight?"

"Stop spouting such drivel," she muttered. "You know darn well that you're just trying to get even with me for daring to oppose you."

Clint's gaze narrowed on her mutinous features. "Are you referring to our engagement as drivel?"

"I . . . of course not," she stammered, suddenly noticing the cold anger in his eyes.

"Good," he murmured with deceptive softness. "Because you've well and truly compromised yourself, Angel."

With a defiant toss of her head, she muttered, "I don't see how."

"You've promised to marry me," he reminded her with a leer to match Snoopy's, "and until you do you're not setting one foot off this ranch."

Her eyes grew stormy. "You can't keep me a prisoner here."

"They were your words, not mine."

She couldn't refute his logic, but she didn't have to concede him total victory. "That doesn't mean I'm not entitled to some privacy, Clint. This is my room and I want you out of it."

The fury he'd kept at bay suddenly leaped into his eyes, and Alicia began to make a strategic retreat. I seem to be making a habit of this, she thought in dismay. Giving him the sweetest smile she was capable of through lips stiff enough to double for cement blocks she whispered, "Please."

Either he wasn't listening or he wasn't interested in the belated courtesy, because the hardened determination on his face didn't lessen. If anything it increased with every step he took in her direction, and when the backs of her knees made contact with the bed she sat down with a startled yelp. Instantly she was pushed back against the mattress, for the moment effectively pinned by the weight of his big body.

Alicia had the skill and the knowledge to disable him, but she didn't even try. No matter how much he infuriated her, she couldn't bring herself to hurt him. Anyway, with his mouth nuzzling the soft flesh beneath her ear, all her fighting spirit collapsed with the swiftness of a pricked balloon. When his tongue began to lick its way down her neck she decided it was much more satisfactory to be a lover than a fighter.

With a throaty mew of satisfaction she turned her head and captured that roving tongue in her mouth. Clint's response was instantaneous and he went wild in her arms. His lips slanted over hers with bruising force, while his body grew rigid and more than capable of slaking her inner fire. By the time the kiss ended her breathing was shallow and her hands were roaming across his back.

"You feel so good," she groaned.

Giving her a crooked smile he shifted beside her, leaning on one elbow as his eyes studied her languorous form. "I never thought I could get so turned on by a dog."

The tip of his finger brushed Snoopy's nose and her nipple burgeoned in response. With a low growl he bent over her and opened his mouth, drawing fabric and flesh inside with a sensual murmur. Alicia clamped her teeth together to prevent the cry she could feel rising in her throat. The pleasure his tugging lips were giving her was indescribable, and she looked down at his dark head as she ran trembling fingers through his hair. The strands were thick and crisp to the touch and the tenderness she was experiencing completely overwhelmed her usual restraint.

Alicia knew the power she was placing in his hands, but was unable to keep from expressing her emotions. "I love you," she murmured.

Clint drew back and looked at her with understanding in his eyes, his voice quiet as he admitted, "I know, Angel."

She wrapped her arms around his neck. "I want you, Clint."

"And I want you," he responded with hoarse insistence. "I want you to be my friend, my lover, my wife. I want you to belong to me and to no other man."

Suddenly she was angered by his possessive attitude, viewing his admission as just another means of coercion. "You never give up, do you?"

Hearing the bitterness in her voice, Clint slowly got to his feet. His eyes were brooding as he looked down at her; his manner was suddenly distant. "You're right. I'll never give up, Alicia. Not while there's breath left in my body."

Then he was gone and Alicia rose to a sitting position with all the agility of a very old, very tired woman. With the mechanical precision of a robot she lifted her robe from the floor and heard a soft thud as something fell from its folds. It was a small white tube of antibiotic cream, and with a despairing moan she began to sob.

* * *

Alicia stood with one booted foot on the lower rung of the white fence encircling the pasture and watched the spring colts and fillies gamboling beside their more sedate mothers. Looking like oversize rabbits as they hopped about the green, sweet-smelling grass, their thin legs still slightly unsteady, the babies made the most of their playtime.

With a lingering glance Alicia turned and headed back to the house. As she walked across the uneven ground she threw her head back and absorbed the heat of the early-morning sun. It was going to be another beautiful day, she thought absently, and she only wished she was in the proper frame of mind to enjoy it. Unfortunately during the past couple of weeks she'd grown increasingly morose.

Her life seemed to be moving out of her control and she couldn't quite decide what to do about it. The threatening phone calls were becoming more graphic day by day, and after being on the receiving end of a couple of them she was beside herself with fear for Clint's safety. The police had installed tracing equipment but the man was too smart to stay on the line for long. Although Clint had tried to reassure her and Sarah, Alicia sensed the danger to him coming terrifyingly closer. At times she felt as though she were locked into a guillotine just waiting for the blade to fall.

To make matters worse Alicia was terribly worried about Sarah. Although her godmother seemed to be taking the situation in stride, she was losing weight and not sleeping properly. The only things that seemed to distract her were the wedding arrangements she was making with what amounted to fanatical zeal. At times Alicia thought she would scream if Sarah asked her one more question about her choice of caterers or her preference for color themes. Since there wasn't going to be a wedding, she wasn't interested in discussing the reception or the style of her bridesmaids' dresses.

When she tried to explain this to her godmother, Sarah simply smiled absently and changed the subject. Sarah wasn't willing to listen to the truth, and Alicia certainly couldn't get Clint to cooperate. He was being aggravatingly obtuse about the entire situation, and she was beginning to realize that he'd inherited his stubbornness from his mother. Yet instead of standing firm in her opposition to Sarah's preparations, she had become curiously apathetic. If she didn't soon get a hold on her flagging resistance, she decided with irascible candor, she was going to find herself married whether she wanted to be or not.

Alicia entered the house through the back door, only to come to an abrupt halt in the middle of the kitchen. Clint and his mother were seated at the breakfast table but what alarmed Alicia were the tears trickling down Sarah's cheeks. Releasing her fortifying grip on the edge of the butcher-block table, Alicia rushed across the floor. As she sat beside her quietly weeping godmother, Alicia placed a protective arm around Sarah's heaving shoulders.

Lifting her gaze to Clint, she asked, "What happened?"

Sarah wailed out an explanation before Clint had a chance to open his mouth. "He's sending us away, Alicia."

The question in Alicia's gaze altered revealingly. "I thought we'd already discussed this subject, Clint."

He looked more austere than she'd ever seen him, his lips compressed into a forbidding thinness. Instead of defending himself from the anger in her voice, he threw a piece of paper across the table. With trembling fingers and a feeling of dread, Alicia began to read. The color drained out of her face and sickness clawed at her stomach. "He...he's threatening Sarah, now."

Clint's nod held grim emphasis and there was compassion in his dark eyes as he looked at his mother's bowed head. "I've already called Kevin," he said bluntly. "He's placing two guards on twenty-four-hour duty at his house. I told him the two of you would be arriving today. Jake will drive you to your brother's, Alicia."

Jake was the bodyguard Clint had hired, an older man who was unobtrusive but impressively vigilant. Since he'd arrived at the ranch Alicia had felt more secure, and although she saw the need for Sarah to get away from the mounting tension they were all suffering under, that didn't mean she was willing to leave.

Keeping this in mind, she began, "But I—"

With an abruptness that disallowed protest, he waved a hand toward Sarah. "She's too upset to think straight right now," he pointed out. "Will you help her to pack?"

"Of course, but I . . ."

Clint got to his feet, his gaze holding the warmth of approval. He bent to place a kiss on Alicia's softly parted lips before turning to hug Sarah. "You'll be safe with Kevin and Jane, Mother."

She sniffed, her eyes tormented as she looked up at her son. "It's you I'm worried about, Clinton. You shouldn't be here all alone with no one to look after you."

His smile was tender, but his voice lost none of its inflexibility. "Jake will be here, and I'm not exactly helpless. I can take care of myself. Right now I don't need to be distracted worrying about you and Alicia."

At that moment Jake entered the room and approached Clint. He was a thin man with a nondescript appearance. His hard hazel eyes seemed oddly unexpressive as he said, "I've brought the car around to the front, Mr. Kelly, but I don't like the idea of playing chauffeur and leaving you here alone. My job is to protect you and I can't do that from a distance of several miles."

"Jake is right," Alicia said hurriedly. "If you won't go with us, let me drive Sarah to Auburn."

Suddenly Clint's patience broke and he scowled his displeasure. "Since I hired Jake it's up to me to give him his instructions, and I want to make certain you and Mother are safe," he snapped. "He'll only be gone a damned hour, for heaven's sake!"

Jake's bland features remained expressionless but his disapproval was obvious. "A lot can happen in an hour, Mr. Kelly."

"Hell!" Clint retorted explosively. "I feel like a colt in leading reins."

Jake gave him a rare smile. "I imagine you do, sir."

"Will you quit with the 'sirs' and 'misters'?" Clint muttered angrily. "My name is Clint. Use it."

Alicia couldn't prevent the grin that curved her mouth as she glanced toward Jake. "He practices that autocratic manner in the mirror when he shaves every morning."

To her surprise a rusty laugh rumbled from Jake's chest. "I don't doubt it, ma'am."

"If you two are through discussing me," Clint interjected coldly, "can we get a move on?"

Clint and Jake left together and Alicia turned to help Sarah from her chair. Alicia studied the other woman with concern, noting the dark circles under her eyes and the fluttering of her veined hands. Clint was right to send Sarah to stay with Kevin, she thought, guiding her godmother from the room. Much more of this and she was going to collapse from nervous exhaustion.

"Come on, love," Alicia encouraged gently. "I'll help you get your things together."

"I'm not leaving him, Alicia," Sarah muttered on a sobbing breath. "I don't care what Clinton says. I'm not going to stay with Kevin and Jane while my son remains here alone to face God-knows-what kind of danger."

"He's not going to be alone, Sarah."

"But Clinton said—"

"Since when have I ever listened to him?" she asked with a wicked sparkle in her eyes.

Sarah shook her head, her expression holding admiration as well as trepidation. "He's not going to like it, dear."

Alicia's voice was determined as she retorted, "Then he can lump it. No matter what Clint says, I'm staying right here."

A quivering smile curved Sarah's lips as she sighed in relief. "I don't know why you worry so about being dominated by my son, Alicia. I think he's the one who should be concerned."

As they climbed the stairs together, Alicia maintained a thoughtful silence as she ruminated over Sarah's statement. Suddenly she felt lighthearted for the first time in weeks and she began to chuckle in irrepressible amusement. "You may be right," she murmured with new insight into her relationship with Clint. "You just may be right, Sarah."

Chapter Ten

Jake looked none too pleased as he negotiated the end of the curving driveway, his hands tight on the wheel of Clint's roomy Ford. They were out of sight of the house when he approached the first barred metal gate, and before he could get out to open it Alicia offered to do the honors. Sarah turned around to watch her climb from the back seat, and when Alicia straightened she and her godmother shared a brief, conspiratorial grin.

Once the heavy gate was wheeled back so Jake could pull the car forward, Alicia sauntered over to speak to him through the open window. "I'm returning to the house, Jake."

"I thought one of those suitcases you handed me was a little on the light side," he drawled knowingly. "My orders were to take you and Mrs. Kelly to your brother's, Miss Mason, and I'll do so with or without luggage."

She gave him the full benefit of her dimpled smile. "I'll take full responsibility, Jake. Clint will understand that you had no choice. He knows I never obey orders."

The older man's lips twitched as he studied the militant gleam in her dark gray eyes. "He may have mentioned that to me a time or two."

She gave him a dignified nod, then spoiled the effect by giggling. "I think his favorite phrase is 'that stubborn, headstrong little idiot.'"

One of Jake's eyelids lowered in a wink. "I think there was an 'adorable' in there somewhere."

Alicia blushed, her lashes flickering shyly as she stepped away from the car. But her retreat was halted by Jake, who thrust his head through the open window to warn, "You and Clint stay in the house and I'll be back as soon as I can. I don't like leaving my post, so to speak, but Mr. Kelly didn't give me much of a choice."

"Doesn't it make you want to smack him?" she retorted. "I'm not the only stubborn, headstrong idiot."

"But he's not adorable," Jake responded with audacious solemnity, earning a delighted laugh from Sarah as he put the car into gear and drove away.

Alicia waved until they were out of sight, then closed the gate and began to walk up the gravel-spattered driveway. Throwing back her head, she breathed deeply of the fresh air. Sunlight flickered through the branches of the tall pines on either side of her, casting dappled shadows. After being confined to the house and ranch yard for two weeks it felt good to stretch her legs, and she covered the distance swiftly.

When the house came into view her stride grew progressively shorter. Clint was going to have a fit when he saw her, but it was only to be expected. He didn't like having his orders countermanded, but he was just going to have to get used to the idea that she had a fully functioning mind of her own. She could handle him, she thought staunchly—a recent realization that pleased her enormously.

She took the veranda steps two at a time, entering the house with a smile on her face. "Clint?" she called.

There was no answer and her smile faltered slightly. She stood at the foot of the stairs and repeated the cry. "Clint, where are you?"

There was an empty feel to the house, and Alicia flexed her fingers in annoyance. Jake had advised Clint to stay inside and keep the doors and windows locked but apparently the dratted man was no better at taking orders than she was. She placed her hands on her jean-clad hips and frowned thoughtfully. If she knew Clint, he was down at the foaling barn checking on the mares who were due to deliver in the next week or two.

Alicia found him in a newly cleaned stall, his bare back glistening with perspiration as he ran a gentle hand over the distended belly of a coal-black Arabian. The sweet scent of clean hay mingled with the less pungent odor of the freshly groomed horse, who had her ears pricked alertly as she listened to the soothing murmur of Clint's voice.

"Hello," Alicia greeted tentatively.

She saw the muscles in his back clench briefly before he turned to face her. Oh, my! she thought as she noticed the ferocity of his scowl with inward amusement. He hadn't even opened his mouth and already she knew she was in for one of his more eloquent tongue lashings. She kept her stance relaxed as she readied her mind for battle.

"What in the hell are you doing here?"

The fact that he barely made any sound wasn't encouraging. Clint was at his most dangerous when he was quiet, and she swallowed nervously as she batted beguiling eyelashes in his direction. "I'm staying with you."

"The hell you are."

She tilted her chin and her mouth formed a dis-approving line. "Must you swear, Clinton?"

"Damned right I must," he muttered.

His gaze held a febrile glitter that boded ill for her future health, and Alicia stepped aside as he threw open the stall door. Once the door was secured to the post, he turned to look at her and she shifted from one foot to the other as though unsure whether or not to make a run for it. As it turned out he didn't give her a chance, placing himself squarely in front of her with intimidating ease.

His muscled arms were crossed over his broad chest, his snug Levi's molding his thighs as he assumed a wide-legged position. Alicia gulped in sudden panic, her glance shifting over his body and up to his face. She again swallowed heavily, her panic increasing when she interpreted the savage message in his eyes. "I . . . uh, thought you might like some company," she murmured faintly.

Apparently it was the wrong thing to say, because his voice grew even quieter than before. "Where did you leave the bodies?"

"I . . . I beg your pardon?" she stammered in confusion.

"Jake and my mother," he murmured. "Where did you leave them?"

"They're on their way to Kevin and Jane's"

He nodded and remarked, "I'm going to kill him."

"Now, Clint," she retorted swiftly, "it wasn't Jake's fault. I got out to close the gate and doubled back here."

"Then he should have come after you," he said harshly. "Damn it, Alicia! I wanted you safely away in case Brewster crawls out from whatever rock he's hiding under. Jake was supposed to be following my orders, not yours. I thought he was old enough not to be taken in by a pair of big eyes."

She scowled at the disgust in his voice. "It was hardly his fault that I refused to go with him."

"He could have tied you up and shoved you in the trunk."

There was an unmistakable plea in her voice when she retorted, "Be reasonable, Clint. You just assumed I was going along with your plans. I never said I'd leave and Jake doesn't have any authority over me."

His mouth took on a bitter curve. "Does anyone?"

Alicia moistened her lips with the tip of her tongue, her heartbeat accelerating as she stared up at him. "My... my husband might, if I chose to give it to him."

"That's the key to unlocking the treasure, isn't it, Angel?" he questioned as he studied her face closely. "You'll give yourself, but you won't be taken."

She filled her lungs with much-needed oxygen before admitting, "No one has the right to take away another person's freedom of choice, even if it's done in the name of love, Clint.''

"And I've coerced you from the beginning," he remarked sadly. "It's no wonder you don't want to marry me."

Before she could open her mouth to refute his statement, a chillingly cold laugh reached out to them from the barn's shadowy doorway. "The little lady has more brains than my wife had, Kelly."

Alicia gave a strangled cry and pivoted to confront the sound. When she saw the dull sheen of ugly dark metal held in a wavering hand, she instinctively leaned against Clint as a short, stocky figure approached them. His blond hair and straggly beard looked greasy and unkempt, his shirt wrinkled and stained, but it was his eyes that caught and held Alicia's attention. They were sunken in the sockets and set close together beneath jutting eyebrows. As she stared into their muddy depths his hatred seemed to enfold her and she was sickened by the viciousness of his expression.

With quick, sure movements Clint grasped her arm and drew her behind the protection of his large frame, his voice reflecting little surprise as he said, "I wondered if you'd use this opportunity to your advantage, Brewster."

Thin lips twisted cynically. "Did you doubt me?"

Alicia clutched at Clint's arm, her whisper one of angry disbelief. "You deliberately set yourself up!"

Brewster uttered another laugh, this one more menacing than the last. "You're a real hero, aren't you, Mr. Kelly? It's too bad such a sterling character developed a taste for other men's wives."

"That's not true," Alicia hissed furiously. "He only helped Susan to escape your brutality."

The muscle beneath her hand tensed as Clint muttered, "Shut up, Alicia."

"Now is that any way for a hero to talk to his lady?" Brewster reprimanded with a cold leer in Alicia's direction. "Why don't you come on over to me, sweet thing? I'll treat you real nice."

"Like you did Susan?" Alicia challenged.

Clint turned his head to slant her a warning. "Will you stay out of this?"

"Afraid I'll give you a taste of your own medicine, Kelly?" Brewster emitted an evil chuckle and Alicia's skin crawled as his hot eyes roamed over her tense body. He shifted his gaze to a rope hanging over one of the stall doors and his cruel features reflected a sick excitement. "Yes, it will be a pleasure to tie you up and make you watch while I show your lady what a real man is like."

Clint's voice held little inflection as he said, "Touch her and I'll kill you."

"Ahh, this one means more to you than my wife did," Brewster replied mockingly. "Suzie was good for a few sessions between the sheets, but you made sure she didn't stay around long enough to become too troublesome."

"I never touched your wife."

With a surly oath Brewster pointed the gun at Clint's chest. "You'd like sweet thing here to believe that, wouldn't you? Do you love her as much as I loved my Suzie?"

Alicia gazed in horror at the thick finger resting against the trigger of the gun. The safety was off and just the slightest pressure would... She drew in a deep breath, her body coiled in readiness. Somehow she had to distract this madman before he had a chance to use that gun.

Before he could stop her she sidestepped Clint, moving toward the other man with cautious deliberation. "Put that thing down, you coward. You're big and brave when you're beating up someone weaker than you or threatening an unarmed man with a gun, aren't you? You're nothing but a worm, a low-life bully, a loathsome..."

"Alicia!" Clint groaned, reaching for her.

"Don't move," Brewster yelled.

"...slug," she concluded breathlessly.

Brewster's coarse features contorted with rage. "You're asking for it!"

His hand was shifting in her direction and mentally Alicia began to count. Ten, nine, eight... Just a few more inches and Clint would be out of the line of fire.... Seven, six, five... She was assuming a downward stance from the snub-nosed barrel.... Four, three... Her timing had to be perfect.... Two, one... Her foot sliced the air in a blur of movement.

There was a flash and an explosive roar as the gun flew out of Brewster's hand. She watched Clint shove his fist into a startled face but the angle was all wrong. Alicia felt a terrible burning sensation in her upper arm. She wasn't supposed to be lying down, she thought muzzily, her brows furrowing in concentration. That kick should have been followed by... Alicia frowned just before she slipped into unconsciousness.

Two days in the hospital was enough for Alicia and she smiled up at Clint as he carried her through the doorway of her brother's home. The bullet from Brewster's gun had merely grazed her arm but shock and loss of blood had kept her immobile for nearly twenty-four hours. Although she'd protested her incarceration vociferously, the doctor had insisted on keeping her under observation until this morning.

Both Sarah and Jane rushed forward to welcome her, and Kevin followed with her overnight bag in his hand. "Is her room ready?" he asked his wife.

Janey nodded but gestured toward the family room. "There's no reason to dump her into bed the minute she arrives," she said, her eyes twinkling when she observed Alicia's relieved expression. "I've fixed up the couch with a pillow and comforter."

"The doctor wants her to rest," Clint stated in a clipped tone.

Alicia gazed at him through the thick curtain of her lashes and tightened her arms around his neck. "Please?" she murmured softly.

With amused satisfaction she watched the flush that darkened the skin over his high cheekbones. "All right, but just for an hour."

She didn't bother arguing with him. There was no need. She was enjoying being the focus of his attention and had finally discovered the best way to deal with a fiercely possessive despot like Clinton Kelly. Soft words, languishing glances, provocative pouts...they were all part and parcel of her new game plan.

That it was working was evidenced by Clint's manner. He treated her like a piece of porcelain, as though he was afraid she'd shatter if he took his eyes off her. She didn't mind. In fact the hungry intensity in his expression was better medicine than the hospital had provided.

Her recovery had begun while they were still in the barn, when she'd regained consciousness to find herself held within the circle of hard, protective arms. Jake was handcuffing their sullen, subdued assailant. According to Kevin, Clint's bodyguard had arrived just in time to stop his employer from beating Brewster to a pulp.

While he rocked her gently Clint had been muttering nearly incoherent phrases. But Alicia had heard because she'd been listening with her heart. "I love you so much," he'd whispered into her hair. "Oh, God, I was so scared...so scared, my darling," he'd choked out against her arched throat.

Then later when she'd awakened briefly in the racing ambulance and been frightened and disoriented by the wail of the siren, he'd soothed her apprehension. "You're going to be all right, Angel Face. No one is ever going to hurt you again."

But the most healing words had been spoken that evening, she remembered with a contented sigh. She'd been lying in her hospital room, her eyelids weighted from the effects of the sedative she'd been given. Just before she drifted into a natural sleep she heard a choked sob, and a voice rife with anguish cried out, "I almost lost you, Alicia. I can't make it without you. Do you hear me? I've needed you for so long...so long, my love."

Clint had been with her every moment. Nothing the doctor or nurses said could convince him to leave her bedside. When Kevin and Jane had arrived he'd seemed almost resentful and had even acted jealous of the short time his mother had visited with her. Sarah had been amused by her son's possessiveness and had given Alicia a rueful grin as she waved goodbye from the doorway.

As soon as they were alone again Clint had busied himself straightening Alicia's blankets, fetching glasses of water and generally making a nuisance of himself. But when they weren't talking he had wandered around looking poleaxed, she remembered with inward satisfaction, which was just the way a man in love was supposed to look.

Once she was settled comfortably on the couch she took pity on the exhausted man bending over her. Peeping at him through a veil of lashes, she asked, "Why don't you go home and get some rest, Clint?"

"So anxious to get rid of me?" he muttered tightly, a muscle pulsing in his rigid jaw.

She placed a forefinger against that betraying throb, amused by his evident irritation. "You didn't sleep at all last night."

"That chair was damned uncomfortable."

With the serene composure of a woman who knows herself loved, she gave him a gentle smile. "I rather gathered that, since you've been growling like a ferocious bear all day."

His dark eyes flashed. "Be careful I don't take a bite out of you."

"Would you like to?" she whispered provocatively.

"All over," he drawled, laughing when she flushed to the roots of her hair.

To her relief Kevin interrupted their little altercation with a typical brotherly remark. "The way it sounds to me, the two of you had better not hold out for a long engagement."

Suddenly Clint straightened, his expression stern and distant as he averted his face. "We're not getting married."

"What?" Jane and Sarah cried out in unison.

"What?" cried Alicia just as loudly.

Kevin's eyes narrowed as he stared at Clint's profile. "Come again?"

Clint shot him a pugnacious look. "You heard me."

"I thought I did," Kevin said, his voice soft with menace, "but I wanted to be certain. Would you care to discuss this in private, my friend?"

Alicia gasped indignantly. "Kevin!"

Her brother's eyes were stormy as they met her own. "I'll be damned if he's going to dump you, Alicia. Clint and I go way back, and I've seen the way he operates with women. Once he scores he usually doesn't go back for second helpings, and he sure as hell has had plenty of opportunity with you. The only reason I let you stay at the ranch was that he told me he wanted to marry you. It's a little late for him to change his mind."

Jane's voice rose in protest. "Kevin Mason, are you out of *your* mind?"

"I was a perfectly adequate chaperon," Sarah snapped indignantly.

Alicia's angry yell drowned out her godmother's voice. "You didn't *let* me do anything, Kevin Mason, and whether or not Clint and I made love is no business of yours."

"Like hell it isn't!"

Clint's features darkened with suppressed fury. "Don't talk to her like that, Kevin. Alicia's a grown woman with a mind of her own, not some witless child. If she doesn't want to marry me no one is going to force her."

"But I do," Alicia whispered.

Kevin's temper had flared out of control and his sneering voice obliterated his sister's quiet admission. "It sounds like you're the one turning chicken."

Clint's hands tightened into fists at his sides. "Why don't we step outside and discuss this?"

"Damned right we will," Kevin shouted. "You're not breaking off this engagement."

"It's Alicia who's breaking our engagement."

This time Alicia's voice was much less tentative as she protested, "But I'm not!"

Sarah and Jane stared helplessly at each other and shrugged their shoulders in unison. Kevin and Clint were too busy glaring at each other to notice. "I'm not going to let you bully her into marriage, Kevin,"

Clint stated harshly. "The two of us have interfered in her life long enough."

"That's as good an excuse as any for evading your responsibility to my sister, but you're not getting away with it. You told me you loved her."

"More than life itself," Clint growled, "which is precisely why I'm letting her go."

Kevin's mouth twisted cynically. "A likely story."

"You are not!" Alicia screamed.

Suddenly the room was oppressively silent and all heads turned in her direction. "I'll be the one to decide my own future," she warned in a more moderate tone.

Clint gestured toward Kevin, his expression disgusted. "That's precisely what I'm trying to tell this closed-minded idiot."

"You're the one who's closed-minded," she snapped in frustration. "If you weren't, you'd know that I want to marry you, you big ape!"

Her revelation left Clint dazed. "You do?"

"Of course she does," Kevin responded smugly. "That's why you're not breaking off your engagement."

"Shut up, Kev," Clint murmured, his eyes glued to Alicia's face.

Tears of joy were trickling down Sarah's cheeks as she quietly left the room. Kevin was too involved in his argument to notice her departure. "You can't—"

A smiling Jane grabbed her blustering husband's arm and began to lead him away. "Shut up, Kevin," she remarked on a gurgle of laughter, gesturing toward the couch where Clint and Alicia were locked together in a torrid embrace. "I don't think we're needed here."

"The jackass could at least have waited until they were alone," Kevin complained in embarrassment as he trailed after his wife.

Clint lifted his head and smiled adoringly down at the woman in his arms. "Are you certain you want to take me on?" he questioned doubtfully.

Unable to bear this uncharacteristic humility in her beloved tyrant, Alicia nodded her acceptance of all marriage to him would entail. She would be bullied and badgered and fussed over, but above all she would be loved and needed with a passion to match her own. Uttering a breathless murmur she rested her head against his broad chest, perfectly content to remain this man's guardian angel for the rest of her life.

* * * * *

Silhouette Desire®

CHILDREN OF DESTINY

A trilogy by Ann Major

Three power-packed tales of irresistible passion and undeniable fate created by Ann Major to wrap your heart in a legacy of love.

PASSION'S CHILD — September

Years ago, Nick Browning nearly destroyed Amy's life, but now that the child of his passion—the child of her heart—was in danger, Nick was the only one she could trust....

DESTINY'S CHILD — October

Cattle baron Jeb Jackson thought he owned everything and everyone on his ranch, but fiery Megan MacKay's destiny was to prove him wrong!

NIGHT CHILD — November

When little Julia Jackson was kidnapped, young Kirk MacKay blamed himself. Twenty years later, he found her... and discovered that love could shine through even the darkest of nights.

Silhouette ❦ *Romance*

COMING NEXT MONTH

#616 TO MARRY AT CHRISTMAS—Kasey Michaels
Elizabeth Chatham wasn't looking for romance...until she met
dynamic Nicholas Lancaster and fell head over heels. Would
wedding bells harmonize with sleigh bells?

#617 AFTER THE STORM—Joan Smith
Aspiring writer Susan Knight was more than curious about her
mysterious new neighbor, Dan Ogilvy. She had to discover what
the sexiest man she'd ever met was up to....

#618 IF DREAMS WERE WILD HORSES—Adeline McElfresh
Ana-Maureen Salem thought she was fenced into her city life. But
then she bought a wild horse and met Jeremy Rodriguez—the one
man who could let her passion run free!

#619 THE KERANDRAON LEGACY—Sara Grant
The legacy of a magnificent Breton mansion stood between them,
but one magical moonlit night Christie Beaumont lost her heart
forever to devastating Luc Keraven....

#620 A MAN OF HER OWN—Brenda Trent
Widow Kaye Wilson dreamed of building a life for herself and
her daughter—without the help of a man. Then she met
irresistible Whit Brooks....

#621 CACTUS ROSE   Stella Bagwell
Years after he'd left her, rugged Tony Ramirez returned to help
lovely Andrea Rawlins save her ranch. Could Andrea risk loving
this masterful Texan again?

AVAILABLE THIS MONTH:

FOUR UNIQUE SERIES
FOR EVERY WOMAN YOU ARE..

Silhouette Romance

Love, at its most tender, provocative,
emotional... in stories that will make you laugh and
cry while bringing you the magic of falling in love.

Silhouette Special Edition

Sophisticated, substantial and packed with
emotion, these powerful novels of life and love will
capture your imagination and steal your heart.

Silhouette Desire

Open the door to romance and passion. Humorous,
emotional, compelling—yet always a believable
and sensuous story—Silhouette Desire never
fails to deliver on the promise of love.

Silhouette Intimate Moments

Enter a world of excitement, of romance
heightened by suspense, adventure and the
passions every woman dreams of. Let us
sweep you away.